Shockproof's mother was  back on code.

She was spreading the word about Ellie and Ann, and he felt sad for a moment. He had been at their home in Westport often in the summer, swimming in their pool, down by the river with Ellie, and feeding their ducks. He wondered who it was Ellie was running off with, if it was someone he knew. Periodically there would be a reshuffle. Susan would come for Christmas drinks with Linda, instead of Francine. Francine would appear some months after with the one Linda had lived with in Maine three years ago. He had once overheard his mother remark that gay life was like musical chairs, only you lived for a few years with what you stood in front of when the music stopped.

SHOCKPROOF SYDNEY SKATE

"From humorous to hilarious . . . a very funny novel about our current preoccupation with sex and what it is doing to us."
—*Publishers Weekly*

MARIJANE MEAKER has written many suspense novels under the pseudonym of Vin Packer and many young adult novels. She lives in New York City.

shockproof
sydney skate

by marijane meaker

A PLUME BOOK

PLUME
Published by the Penguin Group
Penguin Books USA Inc., 375 Hudson Street, New York, New York
10014, U.S.A.
Penguin Books Ltd, 27 Wrights Lane, London W8 5TZ, England
Penguin Books Australia Ltd, Ringwood, Victoria, Australia
Penguin Books Canada Ltd, 2801 John Street, Markham, Ontario,
Canada L3R 1B4
Penguin Books (N.Z.) Ltd, 182-190 Wairau Road, Auckland 10, New
Zealand

Penguin Books Ltd, Registered Offices: Harmondsworth, Middlesex,
England

Published by Plume, an imprint of New American Library, a division
of Penguin Books USA Inc. This work was originally published by
Little, Brown and Company.

First Plume Printing, December, 1990
10 9 8 7 6 5 4 3 2 1

℗ REGISTERED TRADEMARK—MARCA REGISTRADA

Library of Congress Cataloging-in-Publication Data

Kerr, M. E.
    Shockproof Sydney Skate / Marijane Meaker.
        p.   cm.
    "A Plume book."
    ISBN (invalid) 0-04-526539-8 : $7.95
    ISBN 0-452-26539-8 (pbk.)
    I. Title.
[PS3561.E643S56   1990]
813'.54—dc   90-7900
                                                                CIP

Printed in the United States of America

For Nelson and Deb

shockproof
sydney skate

1   *shockproof*

Shockproof's mother was talking in code again. This time the code was not for his benefit. Home from work with flu, M. E. Shepley Skate was in her room, across the hall from Shockproof's, talking on the phone.

The code was for the benefit of the Francher Publishing switchboard, and any of Judy Ewen's colleagues at Francher who might be within earshot.

M. E. Shepley Skate said, "Elliot's moving out tonight and Ann's a mess."

It was a very simple code which Shockproof had broken some nine years ago when he was eight.

Elliot was Ellie of Ellie and Ann. Ellie was leaving Ann.

Much of the code went roughly this way:

Carl was Corita of Judy and Corita, if the discussion was about Judy and Corita. But if the discussion was about Judy and Judy's drinking, Judy could become Judd, as in the sentence "I had a hell of a time getting Judd out of the Running Footman last night."

George was Gloria of Gloria and Liz, but Liz could easily become Lew if they weren't talking about Gloria and were discussing Liz's old affair with the wife of a famous politician.

Conversely:

Edie was Eddie of Eddie and Leonard.

Mary was Martin of Martin and Ralph.

Vicki was Victor of Victor and Paul.   .

But if it were Eddie, Martin or Victor talking, Leonard, Ralph and Paul could quickly become Laura, Ruth and Pauline.

On and on.

Shockproof's nickname for himself — and he was the only one to know he called himself Shockproof — had been inspired by the fact he had known about his mother for as long as he could remember, unbeknownst to M. E. Shepley Skate herself.

Even as early as his third year he had shown an uncanny appreciation of the fact something was radically wrong with his home life: he locked in any male delivery man who happened by with groceries, drugs or cleaning.

Shortly after this phase, he met his father, Harold Skate, for the first time. Subsequently, he spent three or four weeks out of every year with him.

A few months ago he had written to tell his father he was considering skipping Cornell, where in the fall he was to begin the study of zoology and veterinary medicine, and starting then and there in the swimming pool business — Skate & Son of Doylestown, Pennsylvania. He would forgo his college education for an equal partnership with his father commencing 1 July. He had figured out an advertising campaign built around the slogan "Swim with Skates," and saw no reason why they couldn't double the company revenue minimum in six months' time.

On and on.

All people write letters very late at night they wish they'd never written, but Shockproof regularly wrote such letters during the daytime, and the one detailing the future of Skate & Son was one of them. It was due to another Estelle Kelly rejection at Easter vacation.

He could make the most careful, sensitive and gentle love to Estelle Kelly, and no matter how he played it the next morning, even if he managed to remember to put on his shorts so she did not wake up and see *it* first thing, he was treated as though at some point in the night he had defecated on her.

That Easter Sunday of the letter-writing to his father, he had been beaten down by her again. Walking away from East End Avenue, sex smells all over his mouth and hands, since an Estelle Kelly Morning After Frost shattered any notion of taking the time to use the toilet for anything but the toilet, Shockproof had passed churches and heard hallelujahs and decided the only place he would ever be the recipient of any normal love was off in Doylestown, Pennsylvania, where no one spoke in code and life was simple.

"What's this about writing your father you're not going on to college?" his mother had said while they were having a fast one at Kennedy, the morning she met his plane. That was three weeks ago. He had just graduated from a prep school in Staunton, Virginia. His mother had not attended the ceremonies, because his stepmother refused to be present where she was, and Harold Skate had insisted on seeing his son receive his diploma, since he had contributed to its cost. Pointed out by H. Skate in an angry mid-May exchange between H. Skate and M.E.

"What's all *what* about that letter?" Shockproof shrugged.

"No thought goes unwritten, does it, ducks?"

"Oh, some do."

"You ought to know better than to get him all revved up. He thought he'd finally convinced you to chuck the whole zoo scene, to sell swimming pools with him! Skate & Son." She smiled and sighed and took a jolt of her double Old Forester on the rocks.

Shockproof gave a guffaw and said, *"No way,"* and

played the game with himself that the others in the airport lounge suspected she was his older woman.

M. E. Shepley Skate was the casting director of a large ad agency. She had long light-brown hair and bright green eyes, and that morning she was all in white, with a green, yellow and blue scarf stamped YSL, smelling of some great scent that usually poured out of the ventilators in the stores near Fifty-seventh and Fifth.

That was when she told him, "I bought you a graduation gift, a '57 T-bird."

Shockproof was Colette's Cheri, the boy lover, spoiled by the woman whose pearls he played with on her silk chaise. He proceeded with his fantasy at such a pace he was incapable of appreciating the fact that at last he had his own car. He imagined all eyes were slyly watching, ears straining to hear him say, "You bought me a Thunderbird?"

"You know the model with the porthole windows?"

He nodded, affected an effete expression for his audience.

M.E. said, "But the owner won't let you have it for three weeks."

"Thank you. Really," he said, and she gave him a quick, curious glance, which made him wonder if she guessed how often he slipped in and out of his little roles.

She shrugged. "I'm saving wear and tear on my Mercedes."

Instantly the fantasy dissolved. He was an aimless

snob. "You have the Mercedes?" he exclaimed, his voice and face back to normal medium cool, bordering on warm. It took time for him to feel like himself again, after he was separated from her the months he was away at school; he was coming around. "Did you drive it out?"

"I did. Lovely."

"What color?"

"Why would I be all in white? White."

They had another fast one. He glanced around to see if anyone was watching them. No one was. "Thanks," he said, sounding like his old self. "That's a great graduation gift — a T-bird."

He was home.

Driving in from the airport, sitting so he could study her in profile chain-smoking her Gauloises, he wondered if he felt anything for her at all. When he was six through ten and a half, the inevitable four and one half years of his mother's domestic relationships, he remembered fearing she would die, so badly some nights he stayed awake and worried over it. What he feared was that he wouldn't cry at her funeral, and then Lenore Cappenquill would be proven right at last. Cappy always said he didn't care a damn about his mother, not a damn — just about one person: Sydney Skate.

He was always pondering the notion that this was highly possible, when he was not reminding himself that it was Voltaire who said of self-love: it is necessary to us, it is dear to us, it gives pleasure, and we must conceal it.

Of all the women his mother had ever been with, Cappy

was the most formidable. She was an architect, with the offbeat habit for an architect of reading novels the way someone over three hundred pounds ate. That is: Cappy read anything, everything, indiscriminately, from Grace Metalious to Lawrence Durrell — set any book before her, and Lenore Cappenquill devoured it.

From her, Shockproof had acquired his compulsion to read everything on the best-seller list, anything plugged on radio and TV, and whatever was stocked by the rental libraries. He used to compete with Cappy, try to read more than she did and trap her in the mornings at breakfast with a reference to one she hadn't read. He was seldom successful. He was a slow reader, for one thing; for another, he was caught up with an irresistible impulse to memorize long scenes and passages in an effort to embarrass Cappy, who rarely even remembered the names of characters. Cappy called this making wall-to-wall carpeting out of a throw rug, but the truth of the remark did nothing to change his reading habits.

Today was his day off. He had a summer job at Zappy Zoo Land, on Fourteenth Street, Wednesdays off because he worked on Saturdays. Mr. Leogrande, who owned Zappy Zoo, often left it for him to feed some of the animals after six — those which required special care in quiet circumstances — and Shockproof accepted this encroachment uncomplainingly, walking down from Gramercy Park those evenings, and letting himself in to check on things. He was like a Jewish mother with the animals, on the lookout for slobbers in the rabbits, signs of *Ichthyophthirius* in the aquarium, parrot fever, puppy worms, feline hairballs; Wednesdays he worried that in his absence Zappy Zoo would sell one of its snakes to Lorna Dune, an exotic dancer, who regularly taped them at both ends before her performance, often forgot to un-tape them afterward, and then reappeared to purchase new ones.

Shockproof, on this day off, was reading *The Life of Insects* by V. B. Wigglesworth, *Siam Miami*, and *Love Machine*. . . . He was also trying to compose a letter to Estelle Kelly, due home from boarding school any day.

Shockproof's mother was finished talking with Judy alias Judd Ewen, and was now calling her office.

The whole agency was in a flap over who to get to suc-ceed Celeste Skinner McRee as the next Chew-zee girl. High society endorsing gum, not an easy persuasion, though M.E. had already delivered two others from the Social Register.

M.E. wanted a client's memo on the subject sent to her by messenger. The client was complaining about the Wasp tone of the commercials. "What do you mean, he wants more color? That old bone again!" she was shout-ing. "Send the memo down to me! . . . . What do you mean, it's too late? If you know where it's at, ducky, you'll have someone here with that memo a half an hour ago!"

Shockproof was writing:

. . . *simply not going to take your mouth anymore, Estelle. What kind of an impression do you think you make on some-*

one when you say things like "Aw, let's get pissed and get into the hay"? It is just that sort of thing that disgusts . . .

He wadded up the letter and started over.

Dearest. Listen. Carefully.

No. That was his mother at the start of things.

He was at the end of things with Estelle Kelly. Why would he want to continue with someone who had her mouth? In four years at Virginia Preparatory School, he had not come across one boy whose mouth was a match for Estelle Kelly's.

My dear Estelle,
In evaluating our relationship, I have grown to appreciate the fact you are a very unusual person who has been hurt so deeply, your obscenities are a cover-up for certain feelings. I don't even mind your obscenities. You, in turn, should not mind a male's naked body and his normal desire to hear an occasional term of endearment, or his wish to be reassured that you . . .

It was pathetic and he could not humiliate himself that way.

He added it to the others in the wastebasket and began once more.

Estelle,
Allowing me to do whatever I want to do in bed with you is not sufficient for my satisfaction, but then, ducky, if you'd known what was sufficient for my satisfaction, you'd have . . .

He gave up. He tried *Love Machine*, then *The hawkmoth Deilephia can distinguish the blue-violet-purple colors of the flowers on which it feeds . . .*

He could not concentrate. The pandemonium being created in the opposite room over a potential Chew-zee candidate was unsettling. He had a fantasy of seducing Carter Burden's wife, Ba, and persuading her to endorse Gun Gum, while his mother stood by on the qui vive to the whole thing, smiling out of the side of her mouth, shaking her head and murmuring: *"Incroyable!"*

He toyed with the idea of writing a poem to Estelle Kelly. The trouble was he was not in any frame of mind to write poetry. . . . If he did not come up with something fast in the way of a letter or a poem, something, he was not going to have any kind of sexual summer.

He grabbed his Viking edition of Leonard Cohen and flipped through it until he found his favorite Cohen. It was called "MARITA."

> *Marita*
> *Please find me*
> *I am almost 30*

He changed the thirty to twenty in his mind, and took advantage of the fact his mother was temporarily off the phone and in the bathroom. He asked the operator for Western Union, and waited the inevitable seven minutes for the call to be answered. Then he explained about placing the message on three separate lines, knowing the telegram would probably come out all on one line, and that anyway Western Union would likely ignore his request to deliver the wire, and phone it to Estelle.

He had to take the chance that she had never come

across Leonard Cohen, but he took it optimistically, since Estelle looked down on poetry unless it was the superficial sort in the middle of some fantasy musical like *The Fantasticks*, where she could not be accused of being serious about it. Then she would weep uncontrollably, and later slap her knees laughing and making loud jokes about its being a tearjerker and the buckets she'd wept.

Still, Shockproof perceived her intense vulnerability, and persisted in storming the fortress. "Another of Sydney's mystifying compulsions," Cappy would say, "obsessed by insignificance."

Being in bed with Estelle Kelly was like being in an elevator with a stranger. No eye contact; no talking.

One of the various peculiarities of his attachment to Estelle Kelly was that he was not very physically attracted to her. She was small-breasted, which he could have suffered, but the most difficult obstacle for him to overcome was her frequent reluctance to shave her legs or armpits.

He was familiar with the idea that many Europeans preferred their women in this hirsute condition. It was Iolanthe, the Greek prostitute in Durrell's *Tunc*, who *believed that men were aroused by an ape swatch under each arm*, yet like Felix Charlock, that novel's hero, Shockproof begged Estelle to shave. Before bed, and in bed, he would often have to think of things and do things to himself to make sex possible, and at times it wasn't possible, but away from her and remembering her, he could feel a

physical stirring that shook through him and ended with a
sick trembling in the tips of his fingers, and a distant
thumping in his innards.

There were two other possibilities why he was in this
condition over someone like Estelle Kelly, beyond the pos-
sibility he had, in his mother's idiom, "crash-landed in
Masochists' Gulch." One was that, like Estelle, he was
green-eyed, redheaded, and freckled. They could be mistaken for brother and sister.

Would you rather be a masochist or a narcissist?

Another was that Estelle Kelly was the first female over
whom he had ever towered.

She was 5′ 3½″.

He was 5′ 6″.

Once when he had undressed her on a white leather
Milo Baughman couch in her father's living room, holding
his hand out to take her with him into the bedroom, he
had said, "Come along, little doll." It was something he
had never said to anyone before, something it would have
been an impossibility to have said. Little Anything. He
often stood with girls whose chins were at his eye level.

Estelle had responded by rolling her eyes back in an-
guish and snapping, "I didn't *hear* that, Sydney Skate!"

Shockproof's mother was back on the phone, back on
code.

She was spreading the word about Ellie and Ann, and
he felt sad for a moment. He had been at their home in
Westport often in the summer, swimming in their pool,

arching down by the river with Ellie, and feeding their ducks. He wondered who it was Ellie was running off with, if it was someone he knew. Periodically there would be a reshuffle. Susan would come for Christmas drinks with Linda, instead of Francine. Francine would appear some months after with the one Linda had lived with in Maine three years ago. He had once overheard his mother remark that gay life was like musical chairs, only you lived for a few years with what you stood in front of when the music stopped, instead of sitting on it.

When the doorbell rang, his mother was too involved with the gossip to answer it.

"Will you get that, Sydney?" M. E. Shepley Skate called out to him. "That's the messenger I'm expecting."

It was not the messenger.

It was Victor of Victor and Paul. They lived one block away on Gramercy Park South. Victor was a free-lance photographer. M.E. had given him the assignment to shoot the Chew-zee girls.

"No one is going to believe this," Victor said, walking past Shockproof. "Where's your mother, Sydney?"

Before Shockproof answered, Victor continued. "She's on the phone. I've been trying to call. Tell her to get off the phone. This is an emergency. A hairy, heaven-sent emergency, and don't *you* leave my sight, Sydney."

"Victor?" M.E. hollered from the bedroom. "Do I hear *Victor*?"

Shockproof started to reply when Victor hurried back to M. E. Shepley Skate's bedroom, chattering away that nobody was going to believe a thing he had to say, but *would* Shep get off the phone!

Shockproof followed along behind Victor, discreetly hanging back a bit, from practice.

"What *is* it, Victor?"

"It's a reptile."

"What?"

"A reptile. Don't ask any questions. Please. I am very nearly hysterical. Alison Arnstein Gray. Does that name register, Shep?"

"I know the Arnstein Gray family."

"Alison Arnstein Gray needs a favor. She needs a favor and you need a favor. You need someone to endorse Gun Gum. You need a beautiful, filthy-rich, respectable, non-Wasp for the Chew-zee commercial, isn't that what you've been telling me? And wait — wait — and Alison Arnstein Gray needs someone to remove the most enormous viper anyone has ever seen, outside of Kenya, from her bathtub. Sydney, are you standing by?"

"Yes." He moved from the hall to the doorway of his mother's bedroom.

"I don't *believe* you!" said M.E., flying from bed. "You must be kidding, Victor."

"I've been trying to phone you for an hour."

"The snake's actually in her bathtub?"

"In her bathtub, in our very building. If it had happened to Paul and me, we wouldn't have survived the experience, neither one of us. She's in our apartment now. She won't call the ASPCA, because she's heard they kill things. The snake is still in her tub."

M.E. said, "Sydney?"

"Yes," he shrugged. "Why not?"

"I've lost my mind, *that's* what's happened," said M.E., frantically pulling at things on hangers in her closets. "What'll I throw on?"

"Too obvious, Shep."

"What?"

"Too obvious, and we don't have time for you to dress. Sydney and I will go there now. Sydney can just manage with that reptile all by his big brave lonesome, while Miss Gottbucks and I sip something *strong* downstairs. Then . . ."

"*I* show up."

"Precisely. I am Mrs. Mary Ellen Skate, my son helped you blah blah, drinks, idle chatter, and incidentally did you hear about Celeste Skinner McRee's participation blah blah blah *blah*. Oh, Shep-tee-doo, there *is* an all powerful!"

Shockproof's mother said, "Sydney?"

"Yes. I said yes."

2   *the snake in the bryn mawr girl's bathroom*

"He's in here," she said, leading him down a long hallway. .

She was taller than Shockproof, with shiny, pitch-black, breast-length hair. She wore a pair of blue bell-bottoms, a tight white turtleneck sweater, and high open-heeled sandals.

Victor was waiting out the snake's removal on the floor below, in Paul's and his apartment.

"The Sternfields borrowed the apartment a few days

ago, while I was up in Armonk," she said. "They were on their way to Europe with their ten-year-old son. I think Mike left this here. He always had snakes for pets."

"So did I," said Shockproof.

"Which I don't mind, but . . ."

"They make good pets."

"This one smells," she said. "He's really super-stinky."

"He's making himself smell," said Shockproof.

"Huh?"

"He's doing it on purpose."

"How gross."

"He does it on purpose." Shockproof became hotly aware of the fact she had very large breasts for such a tall, thin girl.

"Like a skunk?"

"A skunk will spray *you* with a smell. A snake just gives off a smell when he's afraid."

"In here," she said.

Shockproof had never seen such a bathroom. Gleaming wall mirrors, marble-topped cabinets with white wood-paneled doors and gold rosette knobs, enclosing twin sinks with gold faucets, twin gold candelabra wall lamps, wallpaper depicting a genteel demoiselle handing a flower to a kneeling knight, and the sliding glass doors concealing behind them the tub and shower and snake.

He was a little over three feet, hissing with outrage. His coat had a healthy gloss, and he had a coal-black shiny head. His throat and neck were milk white, while all down his body to the tip of his tail, he was painted with black and white crossbands which connected, so that the pattern resembled a chain.

"See? He's super-stinky."

"He'll stop doing it soon." Shockproof leaned down and picked him up. The snake struggled as he held him.

"He's beautiful," Alison Arnstein Gray said.

"Do you really like snakes?"

"I think they're incredible."

"I thought you'd be climbing the walls."

"That's Victor, not me."

"Oh-oh. This snake is a lady."

"Fantastic! I never thought of that."

"A real lady."

"Pregnant?"

He laughed. "Is that your idea of a real lady?"

"I just don't want to be ankle-deep in snakes suddenly."

"She's not pregnant." Alison moved closer to him then, and he could smell her perfume. Y. Cappy's first lover, a writer named Liz Lear, always wore Y.

"How can you tell he's a she?" she asked him.

Shockproof showed her, aware now of her long white glossy nails. "Her tail's thin," he said, "much thinner than her body. The male's isn't. And she's larger than most males around the middle."

Alison ran her hands along the snake's body. The King was relaxing gradually.

Alison said, "When I dropped acid out in L.A. last summer, I had this huge thing about a snake curling around the universe, holding it together."

"I never took LSD."

"If you're at all bent, you shouldn't."

"What's bent?"

"You know. Bent. A ding-dong. Super-neurotic."

"I still wouldn't," he said.

He was thinking of Esther and Monk in *The Web and the Rock*. He was trying to remember more about Esther, who was the fatal root of all Monk's madness, *which now could no more be plucked out of him than the fibrous roots of a crawling cancer from the red courses of the blood. At other times the green of that first April of their life together would come back again* . . . Esther was a rich and sensual Jewish woman with pale-green toilet paper in her bathroom, who cooked Monk pot roast and steak. (*"Steak, hey? — I'll steak you!" He does so.*)

"Let's feed her," Shockproof said. "Do you have any live rats around?"

"Naturally," she said.

"She'll settle for four raw eggs."

"Yike! You know how much eggs are a dozen?"

"I'll put her back in the tub to eat," he said. "You *do* have four eggs?"

She nodded. "Hey," she said with a sudden, turned-on smile.

"What?"

"She's calm. You know how to handle her."

"Sure."

"That's incredible. I'm super-impressed."

As she went down the hall to the kitchen, she was Esther

on her way to prepare a meal for him while he shaved. . . . He was Monk shouting at her "Wench! Hussy! Jew!" . . . She was Esther writing the letter which ended, "Save me. I love you. I am yours till death."

If she had any discernible flaws, he had not found them yet. He supposed she had bad legs. Enormous piano legs like Judy Ewen's lover before Corita Carr. Shockproof had once overheard Judy confide to M. E. Shepley Skate that it was a blessing women could go more places in pants, otherwise Judy wouldn't be going anywhere but to the office and back, since her lover hated to dress because of her legs.

To dress.

That was more code.

It did not mean "to dress" in the eleventh definition of "to dress" in the *Random House Dictionary*: to put formal or evening clothes on; nor even in its twenty-ninth definition "to dress up": to put on one's best or fanciest.

To dress meant to wear a skirt or a dress as opposed to pants.

In the old days before pants were so popular, back when Cappy was with M.E., Shockproof would hear his mother and Cappy and their friends having long discussions over drinks about where they could/could not go for dinner in pants.

Cappy would always have to be talked into dressing. Dressed, Cappy was uncomfortable. She walked as though the sensible pumps she regularly purchased at Abercrombie's were circus stilts, and lugged her handbag about like someone carrying a twelve-ounce six-pack. Dressed, Cappy always wore lipstick which was brighter and thicker than anyone else's. When she applied it, she pursed her lips as though she were going to whistle, and manipulated the lipstick tube like a screwdriver.

"What are we going to call her?" Alison asked, appearing with a dish of raw eggs.

"What do you want to call her?" Shockproof helped her set the dish down in the tub near the King.

"I don't know. I wish I could keep her."

"*Keep* her."

"The upkeep must be expensive."

"No more than a dog or a cat."

"I have a really gross allowance."

"I could get you free frozen mice."

"Would you?"

"If you'd really take good care of her."

"She'd be company."

"What about your folks?" Shockproof said.

"It's my apartment for the summer."

"Do you live here by yourself?"

"Yes," she said, "that was the deal."

"What was?"

"My family promised me if I got all A's, I could live here by myself this summer and take a psy course at the New School."

He said, "Is that where you go to school, the New School?"

"I'm just taking a course there this summer. I go to Bryn Mawr."

"Oh."

"Where do you go?"

"Cornell," he said. "I'm at Cornell."

"Neat."

"What are you studying?" he said. "Psychology?"

"My parents would like me to. I'm just taking a course in it this summer. The undergraduate psy courses at Bryn Mawr are boring. I'm a Phil major."

"I might very well become a herpetologist."

"That's super, Sydney. What is it, exactly?"

"An authority on snakes."

"Fantastic!"

"I might."

Shockproof stole another look at her breasts and figured she was not wearing a bra. She would be at least 36C if she were to wear one. He had learned bra sizes when his mother had fights with Cappy, and one day accused Cappy of running off with "the first 36C who comes your way." M.E. was a 34A and not happy about it.

"Hey," said Alison. "Guess what?"

"Hey," she said again. "The smell's stopped."

He smiled. He was remembering a scene from *Rabbit Run* when the hero was making love to the whore. The whore got on top of him, and he said "Hey."

"I really want to keep her," said Alison. "It would make up for all the snakes my mother beat to death with hoes up in our garden in Armonk."

"Nobody ever just chases one away," Shockproof said.

"And my *grandmother!* You ought to see my grandmother kill a snake. She really hacks it up. She says if you don't, they split in half and grow into two snakes then. My grandmother's super-stupid!"

"Super-stupid," Shockproof agreed.

"I don't think I can afford a snake."

"Anyone can afford a snake."

"I'll need equipment. What about the equipment? I don't think I can afford a lot of equipment."

"I'll help you," Shockproof said. "I'll make a cage for it, if you really take good care of it."

"Would you? Really?"

"Sure."

She laughed. Definitely did not have on a bra. Breasts shook while she laughed and Shockproof felt something sink in his stomach.

"I'm going to keep her!" Alison announced. "This is incredible! I'll have my own snake."

Shockproof said suspiciously, "Your mother and grandmother won't come here to visit, will they?"

"They promised. It's my place. My grandmother's in L.A., anyway. She lives in L.A."

"Do your mother and father live here in the winter?"

"Part of it."

"Nice," he said, imagining himself all summer long walking over from Nineteenth Street carrying things with him: one night that chilled Lancers his mother liked, and the hard yellow cheese M.E. shopped for on Bleecker

Street; another night Poison-Free Heat-N-Eat Delicacies from the Bio-Organic Kitchen — the poems of Leonard Cohen (were they too bent?), the *I Ching,* some Zap Comix, an Ike and Tina Turner album, *Ecotactics: The Sierra Club Handbook for Environment Activists* — walking some nights in pouring rain so she would have to hang his coat up (beside his pajamas) in the bathroom to dry, and he would kiss her with his head still soaked, her warm fingers with their glossy white nails tangled in his wet hair. "Very nice," he said.

"You haven't even seen it," she said.

"What?"

"This place."

"I can tell."

"It *is* pretty incredible," she said. "Sydney — hey — I'm super-excited. I just hope a snake isn't expensive. I hope I can afford her."

"You can."

"You don't know the size of my allowance."

"I better take it for the night," he said. "I'll take it to ZZL, check on its health, let it rest until we fix up a place for it."

"What's ZZL?"

He told her.

"Hey," she said, "do you want to know something super-suspicious. I just noticed it. Now that you know she's a she, you've been calling her 'it.' I protest, Sydney. That's unfair to women."

Cappy was always protesting ads that were unfair to

women. Cappy had marched against McSorley's Ale House one spring, protesting their policy of admitting men only.

"Last Halloween at Bryn Mawr we burned all these copies of *Playboy* in this big bonfire," Alison said. "Then we all went to the Vomit and had hamburgers and vowed we'd never do housework."

Then she said, "What am I going to name you, Snake?"

He noticed a copy of Rod McKuen's *Listen to the Warm* on the bathroom scale. He had a sudden picture of her immersed in a bubble bath reading poems about ephemeral love, and then she became Faye Osborn from *The Seven Minutes,* telling Mike, "Forget about books and make believe, and let's love each other." . . . *He thrust harder and faster into her, as if trying to weld them into one, and her pelvis lifted and fell with him, and rotated with him, and no more.*

"You could call her Aesculapius," he said.

"Aesculapius was a male serpent," she said.

And then he heard no more because he was telling her inside how it was, he was bursting inside her, shuddering, bursting, letting go and suffocating in her nakedness.

"Concentrate, Sydney," she said.

"I am."

"I want her to have a nice name. Everyone always has it in for snakes," she said. "My grandmother says snakes milk cows if farmers don't keep them out of barns. People are super-stupid about snakes. I identify with snakes for that reason."

"For what reason?" he said.

"Because they get picked on for nothing. They exist; they get picked on. That sums up snakes."

"Call her paranoid," he said.

"Oh, very funny."

"Well, what are you going to call her?"

"She has to have just the right name."

"How about M. E. Shepley Skate?" said a familiar voice.

She was standing at the other end of the hallway, with the YSL scarf tied under her hair, a Gauloise between her fingers. She was in one of her Lilly's, and a pair of Swedish clogs at the end of long, brown, bare legs.

"I knocked but you didn't hear me," she said. "I'm Sydney's mother."

She was carrying the white Mark Cross key case, and he tried to fathom why she would drive the Mercedes just around the corner.

3   *rejection diarrhea*

The errand Shockproof's mother had invented to get rid of him was for Shockproof to help Ellie Davies move some suitcases to the Algonquin, then bring her back to Nineteenth Street for dinner.

It was the first time M. E. Shepley Skate had ever allowed him to drive the Mercedes, and like any first Shockproof could remember, it was riddled with disappointment.

The first time Shockproof had ever had a girl was the

summer he was fourteen, when his mother had the cottage with Corita Carr at Fire Island Pines. The girl was Loretta Willensky, whose father was the famous hairdresser, Mr. Boris. She and Shockproof had been thrown together a lot that summer. They were the only teenagers on that part of the island. When they finally got around to sex, Loretta Willensky kept up a running commentary dealing with her incapacity to feel sensation in the erogenous zones, while Shockproof pumped away on her immobile body like a necrophile.

Shockproof had not wanted to leave Alison Gray's, and for a moment after his mother's arrival while she took charge in M. E. Shepley's inimitable style, Shockproof had veered away from any environment where women were allowed, checked Cornell off and enlisted in the Air Force Academy, reveling in the familiar camaraderie of men with men, enveloped in footlockers, shoe trees, jockstraps, styptic pencils, military brushes, Vitalis, tobacco pouches, until he could smell a heady stew of Mennen's, Jade East, Brut, English Leather, and then hear the high and zealous sound of a full male chorus caroling at Christmas.

Next he was out on the street with the snake, the keys to the Mercedes in one pocket, a package of Marlboros in the other. The latter had been pressed into his hand by Alison, while Shockproof's mother was out in the hall summoning Victor from his apartment.

"I don't smoke," Shockproof had told Alison.

"Those are Mary Jane Marlboros. They're packed with pot."

Shockproof rolled his eyes back and said "Hey. Hey" to show his appreciation, though he had never really felt any more sensation than Loretta Willensky in her erogenous zones, the first and only time he had smoked marijuana. That had been another flaw-filled first.

Shockproof had deposited the King at ZZL and done Ellie's errand, hardly conscious of the impression he was making behind the wheel of the Mercedes. He was veering between anger at M. E. Shepley Skate, and someone named Raoul who had called Alison on the phone.

"Oh, *Raoul!*" she had exclaimed at one point, in a pretense at outrage but grinning evilly, and Shockproof had hated him for having such a cool name and the privilege to say whatever intimate things he had said.

When Shockproof returned with Ellie, there was a message on the answering service that Estelle Kelly was home and expecting him any time after eight.

Shockproof decided to be realistic: that was where his summer was at. Estelle Kelly.

"Ellie, Ellie dear," said M. E. Shepley Skate, when she arrived with some chilled Lancers under one arm, clapping the other around Ellie's shoulders.

Tears formed in Ellie's eyes.

Ellie was a flamboyant 36D professional fund raiser, with that certain aggressive New York female personality, which often started Shockproof off on some chaotic masturbation fantasy in which a woman wearing leather gloves and boots was on top.

Ellie was in a splotchy pink and white Pucci. Her eyes

were swollen from crying, and now M. E. Shepley Skate's presence had reopened the floodgates. M.E. steered her toward the den.

Then she said to him, "Sydney, were you actually cruising that Guggenheim-on-her-mother's-side, paternal-grandmother-Schiff descendant?"

"She wants to keep the snake," he said.

"Ellie? Can you eat an onion pizza from Rocky Lee's?" M.E. called into the den.

"Anything!" Ellie called back. "May I use your phone?"

"Do you have to ask?" M.E. shouted. Then, "Never mind the snake. You were cruising her, Sydney, don't try to put one over on your old Ma. And her great-aunt married a Kuhn, of *the* Kuhns."

"Who'd you get to research her so fast?"

"*Who's Who* . . . When did Estelle Kelly lose her magic?"

"I'm going up there tonight . . . Did Alison agree to do the gum ad?"

"We didn't discuss it."

"Yet," he said.

"Yet," she said. "I think she will."

"Why would someone like that want to sell chewing gum on television?"

"Someone like that was complaining about her allowance."

"Isn't she a little young to have financial problems?"

"She's nineteen, Sydney."

"Oh," he said.

"Cheer up, Sydney," she said, "Sybil Burton ran off with a much younger man."

"Oh, very funny," he said. "Har de har har har."

"We're going to order a few pizzas from Rocky Lee," she said. "Do you want in?"

"I don't know yet."

"Liz Lear is coming down, and Judy Ewen."

The majordomos called in for the MacReynolds-Davies crisis, thought Sydney.

Liz Lear was an authority on modern music; she had an afternoon radio show called "Liz Lear and All That Jazz." Judy Ewen was a textbook editor.

"I don't know for sure," he said. "I'll let you know."

He went back to his room angry at M.E. If she hadn't even discussed the Gun Gum commercial, what was the big hurry to get rid of him? He had the right amount of hostile vibrations to turn the Rocky Lee onion pizza summit conference into an ignominious failure. Just by joining it for a while in the first place, he knew, it would falter some, for they would all be dying to get their teeth into this new breakup instantly, with the Davies half there to give her side firsthand.

With him present, they would have to use restraint and the code in describing the recent goings-on in their lives.

Liz Lear never hid the fact she lived with Gloria Roy. Liz had been with Gloria for ten years, a colossal domestic record, and code was never used in reference to Liz's home life. But Liz was prone to pretend for his benefit that there could be something significant in the fact she was

often over at Roger Wolfe's until all hours in the morning.
Roger Wolfe was a set designer. The truth about Roger
Wolfe was at one glance as hard to divine as the fact that
turtles have shells. Liz's making something out of having
midnight suppers at Roger Wolfe's was code, and so was
Judy Ewen's penchant for introducing all her female
friends to Shockproof as "Mrs." when he knew most of
them had never married.

Ellie Davies had followed M.E. back to her bedroom,
and he could hear them now, arguing over the fact Liz
Lear had been invited.

"She's always been more sympathetic to Ann, Shep."

"I can't call her back and tell her not to come."

"I can see those icy blue eyes watching me now. It's going to inhibit me."

"Ellie, Liz *isn't* hard. She saved my life when Cappy left
me."

He put on the *Promenade* album and listened to: *You
were there when I was not. I was there when you were not.
Don't love me, sweetheart, or I might stop loving you.*

He needed to develop a cool façade. It was the only way
he would impress an Alison Arnstein Gray. He needed to
take a lesson from *Promenade* and memorize lines like: *It
is true I told you I would love you, And I never did. But
remember I'm forgetful, Little Fool.*

He put Alison Gray out of his thoughts, and remembered how neatly he had fitted with Estelle Kelly in the

scissors position Memorial Day weekend. She had fixed them stingers and put on "Pal Joey," which had orchestrated his thrusts inside her. . . . Where had that come from: "orchestrated his thrusts inside her"? He rarely ever forgot such things. He was best with sex scenes from novels, and could rattle off hundreds, identifying the book and the author.

Convincing himself of his past with women did not help him forget Alison Gray, and now he faced the inevitable speculation. What of M.E. and Alison? It was probably already under way. Nothing overt, nothing even slightly suggestive, but something so subtle it was like electricity you never felt go through the switch, and suddenly there the lights were.

Was he Cappy, having hallucinations about every woman who came within five feet of M.E.? Or worse, the wife of Harold Skate, whose fancy it was that M.E. would fall hungrily upon any female form she'd first drugged for purposes of seduction, including Rosemary Skate herself?

The plain fact was — to put it as he had long ago overheard Harold Skate explain it — their kind is not necessarily predatory, and very often, Rosemary, not even interested in a woman just because she's female.

— I don't know what that means, Harold.

— Rosemary, that means their kind can *pass up* a female, too.

— I've got a big picture of that happening.

— Do you think that's all they think about?

— I'm not interested in what abnormals think about, Harold.

Shockproof decided against attending the do in the den, got up, and turned off *Promenade*.

It would be boring to put himself through all that, simply as retaliation for M.E. Shepley Skate's behavior.

What was he doing to himself now?

It hadn't been that bad.

He had merely been cruising Alison Arnstein Gray like any normal, and his mother had come along in the interest of the Gun Gum account.

He decided not to change his shirt to go to Estelle Kelly's, since he would not have it on long anyway, and she never shaved.

Another reason he was not crashing the den affair, he realized as he headed in to give them the good news, was that it had been Ellie Davies who had taught him to drive. He had been about thirteen when he was invited one summer weekend to Ellie's and Ann's in Westport, while his mother settled another emotional crisis with Corita Carr. Ellie had taken him out to some back road in the woods, in her little Hillman Minx, and soon he was behind the wheel, goosing the car along with Ellie shouting, "Shift, Sydney! Shift, Sydney! Shit, Sifney!"

That Monday when his mother picked him up, he could

do everything but park on a steep hill, and "Shit, Sifney" had become jargon.

He went into the den and kissed M.E. good-bye, frustrated because he could not indicate to Ellie he was sorry about her scene. Airily he blew a kiss to her, saw her look of surprise, and stumbled over a cabriole chair leg exiting.

Then he changed his shirt after all.

He slipped across to his mother's bedroom and reached in the enormous crystal brandy snifter filled with matchbooks for a few to take to Estelle Kelly. He found a Café Chauveron, a Clos Normand, and a Pearl's. Estelle Kelly smoked slender brown cigarettes she ordered by the carton from Nat Sherman's, and liked to flaunt matchbooks from expensive restaurants.

He fished out one more as a bonus. The Grenadier.

He went out the back entrance of the town house, down the steps and through the garden.

At Arnold's Delicatessen around the corner on Third Avenue, he dined on the hot dog–sauerkraut–mashed potato combination platter. He thought about the fact that not only had he never told anyone that Shockproof was his name for himself, he had also never confided in anyone about his mother. The two went together.

The summer of Loretta Willensky, she was frequently hinting at her own problems as the daughter of Mr. Boris, who usually traveled the beach with a cortege of males not much older than Loretta. Shockproof played dumb when

Loretta brought up the subject; ultimately she dropped it.

He sometimes felt guilty over the idea that Loretta Willensky might have badly needed to discuss it with someone, but he could not imagine himself talking about it. Knowing without anyone knowing he knew, was his lifestyle.

In the taxi on his way up the East River Drive to Estelle's, he enjoyed a false euphoria which was like the beauty of the river itself. God knows what kind of things were swimming around that you couldn't see. But he was in a buoyant spirit and kept hearing a soft little "Hey" in his ear, while rushing to Gramercy Park South through another rainstorm with a Rocky Lee onion pizza. ("Fantastic.")

Estelle Kelly lived with her father on the twenty-second floor of a riverfront apartment building on East End Avenue.

Estelle Kelly's father's name was Kevin Kelly. *Captain* Kevin Kelly, since he was an airline pilot, had flown in the Second World War, and liked to be called Captain.

He was seldom home.

Estelle's mother had died when Estelle was eleven, and subsequently Estelle had been enrolled in a boarding school in Virginia. Shockproof had met her at a dance during a Paul Jones. She was sixteen then, and in love with a cadet from Staunton Military Academy. Estelle's father's influence had made her a uniform lover. Shockproof had not even the typical navy-blue school blazer to dazzle her with, since VPS was toned down almost to the point of being dormant. Shockproof got nowhere in the face of the SMA lieutenant colonel, caped, epauletted, sabered, and erectile.

Shockproof had not broken through the barrier until last Christmas. The SMA lieutenant colonel was from Florida. Shockproof and Estelle Kelly took the train which went in the opposite direction. En route from Washington to New York, crazed by Southern Comfort, Estelle Kelly had waited until the school chaperone had retired, then crawled into Shockproof's lower berth, where they did it in four meaningless minutes.

The first minute had been taken up with an attempt by Shockproof to reassure Estelle Kelly. "Don't be afraid."

"Of *you*?" she had hooted.

In the morning, happening upon her in the dining room, their first encounter since their horizontal one, he had achieved a casual "Hello there, Estelle." She had left her Cream of Wheat unfinished and retreated to a Ladies, where she remained until Grand Central.

Phone calls, letters, on and on. Easter vacation; Memorial Day weekend.

Now he suffered the cynical eye of the fat night doorman, combed his hair in the elevator, and rang her bell.

Estelle opened the door, gasped, and then pulled her tired old stunt of slamming it in his face.

"Oh! Oh! Oh!" she croaked, opening the door the second time. "It's my trick."

She liked costumes, and she had gotten herself up in some Slavic-looking thing with a tunic and matching silk knickers. The tunic was grass green with white satin buttons, and she had on white stockings and white satin slippers.

"I leaned out over my balcony today and fed your telegram to the seagulls," she said in a Katharine Hepburn imitation, as he sat down.

Captain Kevin Kelly had hired a decorator who believed the environment should reflect the personality. There was a huge wooden airplane propeller across one wall, and the furnishings were reminiscent of the old "Star Trek" set.

"Is your father home?" he said. "Is he in town?"

"Nay, sire, I am a virgin and alone."

Estelle Kelly pretended to sleepwalk her way toward the bar. "The war hero's in Kansas City," she said.

There was a picture of the Captain on the bar. It was one of those purposeless poses where the subject decides to squat down with one hand touching the ground, as though any moment a gun would go off and begin the track meet. The photograph was inscribed: "Fly to your mark, Estelle. Love, Dad."

Estelle Kelly pounded the bar with her fist and said out of the side of her mouth, "What'll it be, Mac?"

"I don't know yet," he said.

Estelle's father, when he was home, was always whipping up deviate drinks like shandygaffs, sundowners, and Byrrh Cassises. Estelle imitated the Captain. She entertained Shockproof the way the Captain would entertain one of his girlfriends. There was a tier of lighted candles at one end of the room, and the smell of Orange Blossom incense. Over the hi-fi, Frank Sinatra was singing "My Shining Hour." The Captain owned every album Sinatra had ever made, and all the musical comedy albums from the Forties and Fifties.

"How about some Bullshits?" Estelle said. "I'll make a batch."

"No, not a Bullshot."

"Why not? I bought the bouillon already."

"I don't want all that bouillon on top of what I just ate."

"I hope you want me on top of what you just ate, because if you don't, Buster, over and out."

"Just plain Scotch on the rocks," he said.

"Just plain Bill," she began, in one of her compulsive, staccato rhyming sessions, "he's a thrill, he can smell my daffodil. I'll hold still, yes, I will — "

"Wait," he said. "Do you have some wine?"

"*Wine?*"

He took out the package of Mary Jane Marlboros.

"Come to Marlboro Country, where the big C is king," she said. "When did you start to smoke?"

"These have pot in them. Liquor and pot don't mix."

"Dubonnet," she said. "How's Dubonnet?"

"We'll see . . . You want to turn on?"

"I'm a sex fiend, *not* a dope fiend."

"Just to try one time?"

Estelle Kelly shook her head emphatically. "Daddy would *die*," she said.

"Daddy isn't here."

"Yes he is," she said, and sang, "his ma-gic spell is *ev*-ry where."

It was true. There was another photograph of the Captain on the square black translucent table beside Shockproof. It was a head and shoulder shot, the Captain wearing his war hero's uniform complete with medals and ribbons. His cap was cocked at a jaunty angle. The inscription read, "Estelle, in the wild blue yonder my thoughts are with you always. Your loving Pop."

Shockproof held the smoke in his lungs and sniffed it up into his head, getting into it very fast, remembering to do everything he had not done the one time he had tried to turn on at VPS. He became more mellow with each drag. He was soon undoing the white buttons of the green Slavic tunic, and very solemnly touching her tiny breasts. Eye contact, big inner steamy buildup at the sight of Estelle's eyes softening with fear, like an animal's instinctive dread at the sound of gunshot. Choked up, Shockproof stroked her hair and murmured, "Stel. Dear Stel."

"Do something obscene to me fast," she said.

"Don't spoil it," he whispered. "Dearest. For once. Don't." It was the way his mother wrote letters, "*Dearest. Are you leaving me? Don't.*"

"Take me in that bedroom and fuck me until I'm in little pieces," said Estelle Kelly nervously. ·

"Why rush, Stel?"

"*Es*-stelle, *Es*-stelle, *Es*-stelle. Don't try to get intimate, Sydney Skate."

She wrenched herself away from him and tore off her tunic. Then down came the silk knickers, white stockings, and satin slippers. Estelle Kelly was buck naked by the Milo Baughman armchair. There was something unsubstantial and pathetic about Estelle Kelly in the nude, the same as there was about a plucked chicken dangling on a hook in a butcher shop. She picked up her Bullshot.

"I'm heading in for the hangar. How about you?"

Shockproof sighed. "Listen, Estelle . . ."

"Listen to what? Rap, rap, rap, rap, rap! How long can two people rap together, Sydney?"

"Were we rapping over here? We weren't rapping."

"*You* were talking."

"What talking?" Shockproof had roomed for three years at VPS with Joel Schwartz. When he was unfairly caught he often became Joel Schwartz. "That was talking?" said Joel Schwartz. "I said your name."

"Okay. I'm fixing myself another Bullshit."

"I just said your name."

"That's what marijuana does, you know. It turns you into a marathon mouth."

"I just said your name."

"You were embroidering, Sydney. You said 'Dear Stel. Dear Stel.'"

"Oh the hell I did," he said, sniffing more pot up into his head. "I said 'Stel. Dear Stel.'"

"There's no difference." She banged the ice cubes into her drink.

"There's a difference in style."

"Oh fart."

"You just can't make a graceful evening out of it, can you?"

"Noisy fart."

"G–r–a–c–e–f–u–l, Estelle."

"U–p y–o–u–r–s, Sydney."

"You might as well put out the candles and the incense, and good luck with your mouth."

"Did you hear about the commercial for Ex-Lax that Bette Davis made?"

"No," he said. "I don't want to hear it."

"What a dump!" she said in a perfect imitation, complete with wrist twist.

Then when he was way, way into it, she didn't bother him when she opened her mouth. There was no big romantic production. They performed. Twice in the kitchen: once against the refrigerator, the second time with Estelle across the kitchen table, Shockproof standing. He had the fantasy they had their own little ring in some circus and followed the dancing bears.

"Next, the bedroom," he said. She lurched into the Waring Blender. "Drunk?" he said. His voice sounded as though it came from the living room.

"Plowed. Finally a bedroom fuck."

"Finally a boudoir screw," he said, trying to say it as

fast as he could. "Finally a boudoir screw. Silently we go at it in the hay."

"I'm drunk enough to talk tonight."

"Do you want to bet?"

"I'll talk," she said, running ahead of him, doing a little backward-forward kick and skip. "I'll rap away."

He followed her, carrying her drink and another MJ Marlboro. "If you don't talk," he said, "when I write a book about us, my sex scenes will be very short."

"Shit on short sex scenes," said Estelle.

"I'll write things like 'they performed twice in the kitchen' — no dirty details."

"Once against the refrigerator," said Estelle, leaping onto the bed.

"The second time with Estelle across the kitchen table, Sydney standing," he said, diving into the mattress after her.

"Shit on short sex scenes. Try to say that very fast," said Estelle.

"Shit on short sess scenes."

"Shit on short shess sheens."

He was suddenly engulfed by a wondrous wave of affection for Estelle Kelly. He grabbed her and held her firmly by the shoulders. "Listen. Dear."

"What?"

"Dearest. Are you leaving me? Don't."

"Unlock the hangar doors, us birds is gonna fly."

"No." He wanted to be serious, to kiss her passionately. He brought his mouth down hard on hers and heard the crack of their teeth hitting together before he felt the ache in his gums.

He sat back rubbing his finger across his teeth like a toothbrush.

"Go down on me," she said.

"I can't."

"Why can't you?"

"Not tonight."

"Why not?"

"Because I read — I read — " and he began to laugh.

Estelle began to, too. "What?"

"Cup-cup-*Couples.*" He got it out finally, pulling his knees to his stomach, howling. "I read *Couples.*"

"If you keep on reading we're not going to be able to do it at all, Sydney Skate, not at all. Not even a fourth of a fuck, if you keep on reading those books," said Estelle.

"John Updike," he said, convulsed.

"Wh-wh-what'd he write?" Estelle was hilarious. Both on their own highs.

"I can't go down on you because I'd laugh."

"I *get* it, I get it, but what?"

"This. Listen," but he couldn't get it out.

"What?"

"Wait."

"All right, all right."

"Okay." He sniffled and caught hold of himself. "Okay. Here goes and this is a direct quote. *He licked her willing slipping tips, the pip within the slip, wisps — "*

"He did *not.*" Estelle had a hold of her stomach.

"Yes, yes, but wait — wait — *more!*" Shockproof was set off again, rolling, holding onto himself so it would not hurt to laugh hard.

"I can't bear more."

"More. Listen, more."

"No. It's too painful. I can't."

"This is a direct quote. . . . *The pip within the slip. Wisps. Sun and spittle set a cloudy froth on her pubic hair.*"

"Stop! Stop! Please! I'm a human being!" Estelle Kelly was holding onto the bedpost.

"Listen!"

"Help!"

"Listen! . . . *A cloudy froth on her pubic hair.* Now. Here. Here. Listen. *Piet pictured a kitten learning to drink milk from a saucer.*"

"Oh God, I'm dead and in hell."

"Here kitty, kitty, kitty, kitty," Shockproof giggled.

"Meow."

"Here kitty, kitty, kitty, kitty."

"It all comes down to pussy in the end," Estelle Kelly was panting. "Oh! Oh! Please. Sydney, would you run through that pip within the slip thing again?"

"Talk about a *tongue*-twister," Shockproof said, and off they went again, shaking up their insides in helpless wailing fits.

Shockproof woke up in a fetal position, staring at the luminous dial of the electric clock on the tripod table.

Frank Sinatra was singing "Let's Take a Walk Around the Block." It was eleven-fifteen. Next to the clock was a picture of the Captain. He was standing arms akimbo on a beach, wearing flowered trunks and a lei around his neck. Shockproof remembered the inscription. "Ha wa ya from Hawaii. Keep your wings straight. Love, Dad."

The window was open. There was a cold breeze blowing up from the river.

Even if Estelle Kelly, half asleep, would let him sleep over, he would have to get up and call M.E. to tell her he would not be home. By that time, Estelle Kelly, fully awake, would renege on the invitation anyway. He decided not to attempt it.

He curled around her for a moment to get warm, and to wait until he was down just a little more. He was falling; he could feel the burden of reality beginning to press. He smelled a strong odor emanating from Estelle Kelly's armpits and feigned an interest in it as a musky smell of sex. He saw himself ending up as someone people brought their cats and dogs to for him to worm.

Then Estelle sent a stiletto elbow sinking into his liver.

"I wasn't doing anything," he said, clutching himself.

She jerked away from him, far over to her own side of the bed.

"I was just getting warm for a minute," he said.

She heaved a huge sigh of exasperation and bolted from the bed, zapped into the bathroom, and slammed the door.

He went into the kitchen, retrieved his clothes from the various appliances, and dressed.

He went back and knocked on the bathroom door, even though he knew it was more of the same since she had sat him out in the Ladies all the way to Grand Central. "Are you all right?"

He waited and then he said, "Estelle?"

"We give at the office," she said.

He said, "I'll be going then, I guess."

Silence.

"Estelle?" he said. "I'm leaving now."

"Don't make a New England boiled dinner out of it — leave!"

He put the matchbooks he had brought her on the table, and left.

By the time he reached home, his heart was racing and he realized he was going to have an attack of rejection diarrhea.

There was a light on in the den.

Fighting back a wave of stomach cramps, he went by the door and peered in. Peggy Lee was singing "Is That All There Is?" There was a bottle of J&B in the center of the rug, next to an ice bucket and a large, smoking ashtray. Stretched out face down on the rug beside the couch, wearing the same splotchy pink and white Pucci she had arrived in, shoes off, a pile of jewelry beside the bottle, was Ellie Davies, passed out.

Under the bottle was a note:

Ellie. Dear.
Liz and I tried to get you to undress and sleep on the couch to

*no avail. I have a very early appointment with my gum peo-
ple tomorrow, might miss you. . . . You know I want the
best for you. Whatever, whoever it is. Shep.*

He dropped an ice cube into the smoking ashtray, then
rushed back to the bathroom, turning on the tub water to
drown out the noise, and endured the ultimate earthquake
from his intestines.

Afterward, he crept in and covered Ellie with a blanket.

M. E. Shepley Skate's door was closed; M.E. was a sound
sleeper.

He went back and sat on his bed and thought about his
evening and the predictable finale. He thought of Jason's
love for Christa in Ivan Gold's book *Sick Friends*. He
thought of Christa writing those letters to Jason with the
melodramatic openers, *Dear Jason it's high noon*, and fin-
ishes like

> *I kiss you
> And six or seven,
> And love,
> Christa.*

The very same Christa who complained in her diary:
*Gagging, rushed to the bathroom. Couldn't, wouldn't swal-
low it. Didn't feel loving enough.*

Jason had called it *the self-poisoning pursuit of that
which puts you down.*

Shockproof ripped off his clothes as though he were rip-
ping away all vestiges of the evening, promising himself
he would get straight for Alison. That was where his summer was at: A.A.G.

4

the snake / the shrink

Erik Satie was running furiously around the tread-wheel behind Bela Bartok. Shockproof whistled, held up a grape, and called his name. The hamster jumped off, scampered across to him and up his arm. He fed him the grape.

"Very nice," a woman's voice said, "very, very nice."

She was shorter than he was, wearing a blond wig this time with dark glasses. Near her right dangling earring was the tiny, telltale mole with the black hair growing out of it.

"What's his name?" she said.

"Erik Satie."

"He knows his name, too."

"Yes."

"Oh, I think that's marvelous," she said, "simply marvelous." She would butter him up for a while before she worked up to any mention of the snakes. It was Lorna Dune's illusion that her disguises fooled him. He wondered in what sleazy joint she had lost the snake she was now shopping to replace, whether she had just forgotten to unplug it after her act, or if the damage had been done during the act, while it wound around her as she gyrated to the bumpy beat of some freaky quartet.

She wanted to know why "the mouse" was called Erik Satie, if they made good pets, where he had learned so much about animals, on and on.

Then: "I happened to notice that beautiful creature in the glass case, to the left of the door."

"The snake."

"What a beauty he is, all black and white."

"She's not for sale."

"Why not?"

"She's someone's pet."

"I see, I see."

"She's a King."

"And your name is what?"

"Sydney Skate."

"Yes, well, Mr. Skate, I'm Mrs. Dunn."

"Uh-huh."

"And I'd be very interested in a snake like that. Do you ever fill orders for snakes like that?"

"She wouldn't suit your purpose," said Shockproof.

"I beg your pardon?"

"A King wouldn't be right."

"Right for what?"

"You have other snakes, don't you?"

"My son loves snakes."

"Yes. Well. What other kinds of snake does *your son* own?"

"He owns two bull snakes."

"A King would eat them."

"We'd keep them separate."

"No," Shockproof said. "It's too risky."

"Does that mean you refuse to order a King for me?"

"I know who you are, anyway."

"It's none of your business who I am. *I* know who *you* are, and I'm about to report you to the manager."

"You'd just turn your back once and the King would get your bull."

"Absolutely none of your business. Where is the manager?"

"Up front," Shockproof said.

Lorna Dune made a beeline for Mr. Leogrande up near the cash register. Her appearance at Zappy Zoo five minutes before closing time was bad news. Now there would be a minor hassle with Leogrande. Shockproof wanted to be at Alison Gray's with the King by five-thirty. The sooner he got there, the longer he stayed. She had told him over the phone that morning that she had a dinner date. There would be just time to deliver the snake, get the cage set up, and explain to her what she needed to know about her care.

He put Erik Satie back and cringed at the sound of Lorna Dune's angry voice complaining to Leogrande.

So far it had been a good day, too. His Thunderbird had been delivered that morning by its ex-owner, and after that Ellie Davies, who had been too hung over to go to work before noon, had taken him to the Gramercy Park Hotel for a huge breakfast. Both had had Bloody Marys; he had one to Ellie's four. Ellie became vaguely confiding. She said that at one time she had thought rather highly of Liz Lear as an intellect, but she was now of the opinion she was mediocre, though she would withhold comment on Liz as a person, since Liz was still one of M.E.'s close friends.

On and on.

She seemed also to be bordering on tears several times. If she was the one leaving, why was she the one crying? He had never thoroughly understood all these nuances in what he had heard M.E. call "dividing dishes." When Corita Carr had broken up with Ann MacReynolds years back, they had gone to court over custody of a blue-point Siamese. Corita won, then moved back in with Ann for another year. Finally Corita had run off with someone allergic to cats, and now Ellie was complaining to Shockproof that she should have the cat who was currently boarding with Ann.

"If she wants a King, we get her a King," said Leogrande, behind Shockproof.

"She's got bulls."

"That's her problem, Sydney."

"Why do we have to sell her snakes? Business is good, isn't it?"

"She's a customer."

"What you might call a steady customer."

"That's *her* business, Sydney."

"It's ours, too."

"We're not the SPCA."

"Not even close," Shockproof agreed.

"There are a dozen kids who'd like this job."

"And wouldn't be any good at it."

"Sydney, I'm warning you: if she wants a King, we get her a King."

"She wants one. Right?"

"That's what she wants."

"All right," Shockproof said. "All right."

"You're not St. Francis."

"Neither are you."

"I'll lock up. You make a note of the order and put it through tomorrow, and I'll lock up."

"Both new rabbits have ear canker," said Shockproof.

"Did you do anything for them?"

"I put camphorated oil in their ears, but they might need a vet."

"The vet will charge more than we charge for them," Leogrande said. "If there's no improvement tomorrow, we ship them back."

"I'll read up on ear cankers. Don't panic."

"They arrived with fleas, too."

"I'll bet we're the only animal dealers in New York who'd sell her a snake," said Shockproof.

"Write up the order and stop dreaming. We're the only animal dealer in the United States who'd give it a second thought."

Shockproof made a note to write up the order.

Then he carried the wooden cage with the glass front down to the parking lot on Fourteenth Street, placed it in the back of the Thunderbird, and returned to Zappy Zoo for the King.

He was on Gramercy Park by five-thirty after all.

The living room was ornate with thick carpets, antique furniture covered in velvet, a crystal chandelier, a marble fireplace, and a bay window with panes of blue glass, looking out on a garden containing a gaslight lamp near a fountain with water flowing from it.

Shockproof had set the cage near the balcony.

Alison was holding the snake.

Alison did not have piano legs. Her legs were long and thin. She was wearing a very short white linen mini-skirt, a pink sleeveless sweater, and pink sandals with short square heels.

"I still can't think of a name for her," she said.

"She'll only need to be fed once a week."

"Would you mind doing that?"

"You just drop it in really."

"Drop what in."

"A mouse. Mice."

"Oh *no*."

"We have frozen ones we sell."

"Would you mind doing it?"

"I'll do it."

"Is it going to be expensive?"

"I told you I'd get the mice free."

"Neat. Because my family forces me to live like a miser."

"It doesn't look it."

"This isn't my place, it's their place."

"I know," he said. "You told me."

"I have to live on next to nothing. If Raoul didn't give me pot, I wouldn't even be able to afford to smoke."

The telephone rang and she handed him the King. "I want to get that in there," she said.

She went into the bedroom.

He heard her say, "Oh, hel-lo! May I pick you up? I have my car. Oh, no?" Then the door was pushed shut by the toe of her pink sandal.

On the table there was a bright blue spiral notebook with Bryn Mawr College stamped across it in silver, and a silver and blue seal beneath that. In the top right corner in black ink was *Alison A. Gray. Erdman Hall.*

Across the bottom was printed ORGANIC CHEMISTRY.

Alison had been writing in the notebook when he arrived.

He thought she had told him she was taking a course in psychology at the New School. Why was she still studying her old organic chemistry notes from Bryn Mawr?

He opened the notebook to the first page.

I'm so excited and happy! Raoul sent me a huge bouquet of flowers. All I want to do is sit and contemplate them, but I'm going over to Haverford to smoke with Doug. I feel very guilty when I'm with Doug, because I pretend he's Raoul and show him the love I feel for Raoul. It's unfair to Doug, but I can't hold myself back, since I'm a Scorpio, and always super-horny. If only Raoul attended Haverford, but then he would never be the excellent doctor I know he can be!

Shockproof felt guilty and elated.

The notebook was very thick. The entry Shockproof had just read was written over a year ago.

Shockproof looked at the entry under it.

How can I make some extra money? All the calls for baby-sitters are on weekends when I want to date. It is too late to sign up for waiting on table. There is a chance I could push, since the girl who sold me mescaline last week is transferring next semester to Michigan, but I need money super-fast since I have practically no new clothes!

Shockproof flipped to the last page, and read the entry she had been working on when he arrived.

Last week a big 8-hr. argument-conference with my parents. The thing began over their suspicion that I smoke and drop and am closed to them. The fact is I am, if it comes to

*telling them everything. I don't intend to tell them everything.
Just to be able to sort of spontaneous talk with them would be
nice, but they get me too uptight with their fluctuation. One
minute they are all for me and understand my scene, and the
next minute mother says she wished she had raised me differ-
ently and that she wonders where the lack was in her. Great!
To be formed by another's faults! I really appreciated that
one.*

Shockproof turned back to the entry preceding that one.
It was yesterday's date, and Shockproof was looking for
himself.

*Raoul sent me a telegram. "Into the crowned knot of fire,
and the fire and the rose are one." He signed it. "Found."
I returned with "Only the loving find love."
I'm going through a bored phase.*

Shockproof returned the notebook to the table. The
King was curled up between his legs on the velvet love seat
and he took her and put her in her cage.

"I'm super-sorry about the interruption," said Alison, returning from her telephone call. "Hey. Guess what?"

*From her huge shoulders down she is one long under-
belly erect in light above him; he says in praise softly,
"Hey."*

"What?" Rabbit said.

"I thought of a name for her."

"Hey."

She answers, "Hey."

"You're pretty."

"Come on. Work."

Galled he shoves up through her and
"Let's call her Dr. Teregram."

"Why?"

"That's my analyst's name."

"Okay," he said. "If you want to name a snake after your analyst."

"It's super-appropriate."

"Fine . . . Is it a *psycho*analyst?"

"Yes." Her face was suddenly aglow and she clapped her hands and gave a squeal, running across to the cage, ruining his image of her as this cool Bryn Mawr coed out of *Our Crowd*. She cooed, "Hi, Dr. Teregram."

"Did you just start going to this analyst?"

He remembered when Corita Carr began analysis. She used to come home after her session and pour straight double bourbon, drink it standing up in the kitchen, and mutter, "That son of a bitch!"

Alison said, "I started being shrunk way last September."

"Do they analyze you at Bryn Mawr?"

"The analyst comes to Bryn Mawr."

"To your room?"

There was a real mystique to psychoanalysis, Shockproof knew — rules, protocol; it was like a tribal rite. Once at a large sit-down dinner, Corita Carr had remarked that she had discovered she was jealous of the goldfish in her doctor's office, because they never had to leave. The whoops of laughter from everyone amazed Shockproof.

Corita Carr had leaned across the table and said, "You had to *be* there, Sydney."

Alison said, "Oh wow, not to my room," and let out a surprise giggle. "She goes to the infirmary, and I go there to see her. It's staged in the infirmary, just in case you don't suspect you're sick."

"I've never been shrunk."

"I didn't ask to be."

"Did your parents make you be, or did Bryn Mawr make you be?"

"Bryn Mawr never makes you be anything. My parents did. My mother was in analysis for eight years. She still goes back in times of crisis."

"How could she make you be analyzed?"

"By telling me I couldn't go back to Bryn Mawr," Alison said. "But now I don't mind it. I'm getting all these really super-helpful insights, and I think I'm Dr. Teregram's most interesting case, too."

"Nobody in our family's ever been analyzed," he said.

"Where's Mr. Skate?"

"In Doylestown, Pennsylvania. He's remarried."

"That's neat," she said. "My parents don't have the guts to get a divorce."

"M. E. Shepley Skate and Harold didn't make it much past the first month of connubial bliss."

"Hey," she said, "you're neat. Will you mail some letters for me as you leave?"

"Is that a hint?"

"I'm way behind schedule today; it's really gross. I've been on the horn too much."

He walked across to the cage and said, "Well, good-night, Dr. Teregram."

Alison let out another squeal at the mention of her analyst.

Then she said, "I'd smoke with you or something, but I have to be at Elaine's Restaurant by seven o'clock."

She was wearing Y again.

"I'll be in touch," he said.

She reached into the pocket of her mini and took out some letters and a postcard. "There's a mailbox right on the corner of Gramercy South and Irving."

He took the mail. "I'll be in touch," he said.

"Next time we'll turn on," she said. "I've got some Acapulco Gold in the vegetable bin. If I wanted to sell it, I could probably get thirty dollars."

As he rode down in the elevator, he read the postcard. It was addressed to someone in Los Angeles.

Dear Sandra,

It's really gross not to be in L.A. this summer. I miss it, but I am nearer Raoul. Hey. Guess what? Raoul sent me a telegram: "Into the crowned knot of fire: and the fire and the rose are one." From T. S. Eliot, The Four Quartets. *He signed it "Found." I returned with "Only the loving find love," from D. H. Lawrence. Please write what's happening. New York is boring. Ali.*

5 *don't love me sweetheart / i might stop loving you*

It was Harold Skate's practice to write letters on Skate Pool invoice forms. There were two sheets to a form. Shockproof was expected to put his answer beneath his father's message (extending it, if necessary, to the extra invoice always enclosed) — then to rip off one for his own records, and forward the duplicate for his father's files. .

That Friday morning, the following invoice arrived as he was having breakfast with his mother.

Dear Sydney,
Please find enclosed herewith a check for forty-five (45)
dollars. In replying, please acknowledge receipt of this money.
Your stepmother and I will be in New York City on Tuesday
forthcoming, at the Commodore Hotel for a business confer-
ence.
We look forward to seeing you.
Use the enclosed to purchase three seats (one for you as
our guest) to something light on Broadway. Your stepmother
and I have seen Fiddler on the Roof *and* Butterflies Are Free.
Neither of us would be particularly interested in comedies
about the race issue or with nakedness, since this is also a
vacation of sorts.
We had a barbecue for twenty in our backyard last night.
                        Affectionately,
                        Your father, Harold E. Skate

M.E. said, "He probably has a copy of every letter he's
ever written or received."

"What were his letters like to you?"

"Not very different from this one," she said, handing
the invoice back to Shockproof.

"Boy, I sure don't see you two together, at all!"

"Boy, you sure don't," she said.

They usually had breakfast in a corner of the kitchen
overlooking the garden. The basement of the town house
was rented out to two NYU students, Mike and Albert, who
often suntanned in the garden, encircled by the various
sand sculptures Cappy made the summer they had spent
on Martha's Vineyard.

Shockproof had a great deal of privileged information
about both boys. At night he would often not turn on his

lights in his room, and crouch by the window listening to what they said to one another, to others, and about one another.

Mike was the Don Juan of the twosome. He was always making deals with Albert, so that Albert would not return until 2 A.M. on certain evenings. Mike was an encyclopedia of romantic clichés when he entertained a girl. They would be sitting out under the stars turning on after Mike had made them charcoal steaks, and Mike would wait for a moment of silence. Then Mike would reach for the girl's hand and say softly, "Hello."

Sometimes, "Hi!"

Another of his favorites was to wait for a break in the conversation and say, "Mary?"

"What?" Mary would say.

Mike would say, "Thank you."

"For what?"

"Thank you for being Mary," Mike would say.

Sometimes Mike would not say anything, but reach across instead as though he were delivering a slow-motion punch, barely grazing the girl's chin. He might follow with "Glad you came." Sometimes it was put as a statement of fact; sometimes it was a question.

Then there was Mike's psychosemantic side.

"Aileen," Mike would say, "I love you. I may even be *in* love with you."

"Betty," Mike would say, "I love you. But do you know something? I also like you, genuinely like you, as a person."

Albert was the garden intellectual. He romanced his dates by playing Bach full pitch over the hi-fi, and sometimes recorded discussions by Herbert Marcuse, Stokely Carmichael, and Thic Nhat Hahn. If Albert made out, Shockproof had no glimmering of it. He had never even seen Albert holding hands with one of his dates. Albert's women were of the leather shoulder bag, leather sandal variety, with steel-rimmed spectacles, no makeup, and leather watch straps.

Albert prefaced almost everything he said with a so-and-so said, as Dostoevski said, as Terry Southern said, as Martin Buber said, as Marshall McLuhan said; he often sounded like one of the dead Kennedys giving a major policy address, stealing support for his ideas from *Bartlett's*.

M. E. Shepley Skate answered the telephone on the first ring, punching a yolk of her egg with her fork as she picked the cradle off its receiver with her left hand.

"Annie!" she said. "Hi! Love. How *are* you?"

The distaff side of Ellie and Ann: Ann MacReynolds. She was most famous as a female computer in a TV spaghetti commercial, which M. E. Shepley Skate had cast. She said "I'm programmed for Porproganni!" and then a box of spaghetti wearing a black mask and a silver saber waltzed away with her. She also played in various productions at La Mama and New Dramatists.

M. E. Shepley Skate said, "Yes, I know where Ellie's staying, but Annie, is it fair to ask me?"

Shockproof waited to be sent out of the room on the

inevitable errand. He downed as much of his scrambled eggs as he could, while they were still warm.

"I can tell you she's *not* staying with the alleged new person," said M. E. Shepley Skate.

M.E. listened for a while and then said, "No, Annie, she does *not* bring whoever it is here. I wouldn't do that to you, and neither would Ellie. Annie. Love. You know better."

M. E. Shepley Skate snapped her fingers to get Shockproof's attention. She cupped her hand over the receiver and said, "Sydney, would you get me a fresh pack of Gauloises from my purse in the bedroom? Please?"

Shockproof put down his fork and got up. Halfway down the hall he could still hear his mother. "If you think Ellie's taking this any better, you're very mistaken, Annie. Seriously. And I promise you I haven't even met this alleged new person. . . . What? Well, what the hell is she if she isn't alleged? Nobody's met her!"

Shockproof sat down on the bed in his mother's room to give her extra time. He took her purse from the bedside table, opened it, and found the Gauloises. There were several matchbooks from Stay. The front covers said:

> *fay foote's*
> S T A Y

The back covers said:

> *don't go*
> S T A Y
> *don't go*
> S T A Y
> *don't go*

S T A Y
don't go
STAY on 3rd
at 90th Street

In the morning before she went to work, Shockproof's mother always reached into the enormous crystal brandy snifter for matchbooks. The Stay matchbooks were never put into the snifter. Before she went to the office, M. E. Shepley Skate usually removed the Stay matchbooks from her bag and coat pockets.

Shockproof had never been to Stay, but he knew Fay Foote. Fay Foote was a legend in gay life. Shockproof had overheard more about Fay Foote than anyone else. Fay Foote was notorious in au courant straight circles, too.

Back in the years when M. E. Shepley Skate was with Cappy, Fay Foote had been paid fifty thousand dollars by a gay boy to marry him. She had been promised a thousand a month thereafter for life. The gay boy was Foster Foote of Foote Refineries in Dallas. Before Fay married him, he could not come into his inheritance. His grandfather's will stipulated he was to have a wife.

Foster Foote also helped set up Fay in the restaurant business. In addition to Stay, Fay Foote owned Linger in Southampton.

Fay Foote looked like Anne Bancroft playing Mrs. Robinson. She was always rumored to be off in Acapulco with a famous actress, or in Rio with the wife of some famous person. She was always tanned and just back from Tangier, Antigua, Gstaad, or wind-burned and home from St. Moritz or Aspen.

Women were reputed to enter Stay on their husband's arm, and leave on Fay Foote's. Often it was the husbands who took the tumble, but Fay Foote was not AC-DC. Shockproof had heard other expressions for it such as double-gaited, both ways, and bi, but he had never forgotten Fay Foote's way of saying she wasn't like that. Out at Judy Ewen's in Amagansett last summer, while Shockproof was making a batch of mint juleps for everyone, he had heard Fay Foote holding forth out on the terrace. "I'm just not succotash!" she had exclaimed.

That same weekend, when Shockproof was trying to sleep one night, he had overheard this between M. E. Shepley Skate and Fay Foote:

— Sydney digs, Shep.

— No.

— You're out of it, if you think he doesn't.

— Why do you think he does?

— He's not a dumb-dumb, Shep. He knows where it's at.

— Sydney's very intelligent, but don't mistake intelligence for sophistication.

Shockproof put his mother's purse back. He thought of Estelle Kelly. Before yesterday he had always called Estelle Kelly the day after, no matter how badly she had treated him during her postsexual depression.

He would miss Estelle Kelly, and from time to time regret that he had put all that behind him to enter a new phase.

He would have to go to the library and find *The Four Quartets* by T. S. Eliot, in order to discover what this thing was about the crowned knot of fire and the rose.

For a time he sat on the bed trying to improve on yesterday's conversation with Alison. He should never have asked her if the analyst came to her room at Bryn Mawr. Of course the analyst didn't come to the room. He knew enough from Corita Carr's analysis to know the analyst didn't budge for the analysand. Once, back in the time when there were newspaper accounts of people setting fire to themselves in protest over something, Corita Carr had been unable to persuade her analyst to find her some matches, so she would not have to continue her hour without a cigarette. Her analyst refused, saying he did not smoke and had no matches. Corita Carr had begged him to just step out into his apartment, go to the kitchen, and light her cigarette from his stove. Her analyst refused. Corita Carr had groaned at him. "I can't *believe* you'd treat me this way. I could douse myself with kerosene and set myself afire, I'm so traumatized by this whole thing." Her analyst replied, "May I remind you that you have nothing with which to ignite yourself?"

"That son of a bitch!" Corita Carr had said. "Oh, that son of a bitch!"

Another thing Shockproof never should have said was "Is that a hint?" when Alison said, "Will you mail some letters for me as you leave?"

He should have just left. Cool. *Promenade. — You were there when I was not. I was there when you were not. Don't love me, sweetheart, or I might stop loving you.*

Another thing he should never have said was the second "I'll be in touch." One "I'll be in touch" was just right. Two threw things out of whack. He sighed. M.E. was right. He was definitely not sophisticated. He was no Raoul who knew enough to sign telegrams "Found." "Lost" was more his style, and now he remembered the scent of Y, felt his stomach give, and Alison Arnstein Gray, *did first what no one had ever done better . . . well holding arms, quick searching tongue, the flat eyes, the good taste of mouth, then uncomfortably, tightly, sweetly, moistly, lovely, tightly, achingly, fully, finally, unendingly, never-endingly, never-to-endingly, ca-ROOOOOOOOM* — Shockproof blew off his head with a twelve-gauge shotgun. So much for the affair between "Papa" and A.A.G.

Shockproof was almost to the kitchen when he heard the windup of his mother's telephone conversation with Ann MacReynolds.

". . . So Liz and I had dinner with her at Elaine's."

He froze, remembering Alison saying yesterday she had to be at Elaine's.

"I think she needs the money, but she's too well brought-up to admit she'd do it for money. I had to say something about charity and her prerogative blah blah if she wants to donate the money. . . . Are you *kidding*, Annie? Dear, she's nineteen. A lit-tle young."

You child, she gasped, you don't understand, you can't

understand — God help me, I love you. And now she had
the girl in her arms and was kissing her eyes and mouth:
Mary . . . Mary.

When Cappy had lived with them, she had a small
cache of books she kept hidden in the bottom drawer of
her file cabinet. The first one which Shockproof had ever
smuggled out to read was *The Well of Loneliness.*

"Good-bye then, Ann. Don't be a stranger," said M.E.
. . . then, "Sydney?"

"Coming."

"Your breakfast is cold."

"I had all I can eat."

"What's the matter with you all of a sudden?"

"Nothing is."

"Something is."

"Is she going to do it?"

"Is who going to do what?"

"Alison. Is Alison going to do the commercial?"

"I don't know."

"She's always talking about money."

"Are you always standing out in the hall listening?"

"I heard the tail end."

"I was telling Annie: she's only nineteen. That's a lit-tle
young to be thrown into the commercial rat race."

"Or any rat race," he said.

"Shall I make you some warm toast?"

"No thanks."

"Sydney, what's the matter with you?"

"Nothing."

"I know you were cruising her Wednesday, but you don't think of yourself as being *involved* with her, do you?"

"Who said anything about involvement?"

"Because she goes with this Harvard Med. School student."

"Raoul."

"Yes. She told you about Raoul?"

"I heard about Raoul," Sydney said.

"She's been going with him for a couple of years."

"And he goes to Harvard?"

"Yes."

"I didn't know where he went."

"She's too old for you, Sydney."

"Two years older. In December, one year older."

"I don't mean chronological age."

"You mean I'm not mature."

"Sydney, when she was your age she was finishing up her first year at Bryn Mawr. That's all."

"Kaput. Huh?"

"What's happening with you and Estelle Kelly?"

"Kaput because when she was my age she was finishing up her first year at Bryn Mawr!"

"Bryn Mawr is something else, Sydney. Bryn Mawr girls aren't your little Stuart Hall girls."

"Who wants a little Stuart Hall girl?"

"Men stay overnight in the dorms, that sort of thing."

"I'm impressed."

"I'm not trying to impress you."

"Yes you are."

"No I'm not."

"Yes you are. With the fact I'm intelligent but not so-phisticated," he said. "That's your standard appraisal of me."

"Sydney, I don't believe this."

"Isn't it?"

"Isn't what?"

"Isn't your standard appraisal of me that I'm intelligent but not sophisticated?"

"Sydney."

"Isn't it?"

"Sydney, she's not your dish."

"It *is* your standard appraisal of me."

"Whatever happened between you and Estelle Kelly?"

"She's sick."

"What's wrong with her?"

"Not *sick* sick. A ding-dong. Super-neurotic," he said. "Bent."

"Where did you get that word?"

"Bent?"

"That's Alison Gray's word."

"She's one of many who use it, yes."

"Good luck, Sydney."

"What does that mean?"

"You're going to need it."

"That's super-sensitive of you. That's grossly typical of a parent. Alison and I were talking about this very thing."

"Grossly typical. Dear God, Sydney."

"What's the matter now?"

"Super-sensitive and grossly typical."

"What's the matter with that?"

"Don't be so derivative."

"I'm being me myself."

"You and Alison were talking about what thing?"

"Parents."

"Oh?"

"Their fluctuation."

"Since Harold Skate has not been known to fluctuate one iota since the day he was born, you must be referring to your old Ma."

"Nothing in particular."

"What in general?"

"Just the idea one's formed by another's faults."

"*What?*"

"Formed by another's faults."

"Sydney, what *are* you talking about?"

"I don't know," he said. He didn't. Suddenly he had lost track.

"If you've got some legitimate gripe, let's hear it," said M.E.

"I don't."

"Then let's both simmer down."

"Did she call you?" he said.

"What?"

"Did *she* ask *you* for dinner?"

"I told her to get in touch with me if she was interested in the commercial."

"And the very next day she did."

"Yes."

"Greed."

"She says her parents are very careful with a dollar."

"Greed."

"Come off it, Sydney. You'd do it in a second if you had the chance."

"The very next day she's on the horn."

"You really take it all in like a sponge, don't you?"

"What?"

"On the horn. That's her expression, too."

"A lot of people say 'on the horn.' "

"You just started saying it, though."

"I give up."

"Oh, well, Sydney, I'm impressionable, too; anyone with an accent who walks into my office passes the accent on to me like a virus."

"Yeah." He sighed . . . then he said, "Estelle Kelly has a father fixation."

"Well, she doesn't have a mother, does she?"

"There are things wrong with her I don't even care to go into."

"Does that mean it's over?"

"Fini," he said.

"Too bad, Sydney. I like Estelle."

"Did she say anything about me?"

"I haven't talked to her recently."

"I mean Alison. Last night . . ."

"She said you were 'super-confident' around snakes."

"Did she say anything else?"

"Not that I remember."

"She must have said something else."

"She said I looked 'super-young' to have a son your age," M.E. chuckled.

"She's really greedy for that money," he said angrily.

Then Stephen took Angela into her arms, and she kissed her full on the lips, as a lover.

"Dear Miss Dune," he wrote, soon after he arrived at work that morning, "Here at Zappy Zoo Land we have decided there is not enough profit and too much upkeep involved in stocking reptiles, so we have altered our policy to exclude them. I am sorry to inform you of this, but I am sure you will find other dealers who . . ."

He had learned her address by phoning Celebrity Service and using his mother's name. His mother was always tracking down talent for agency commercials.

Lorna Dune lived in Queens. He hoped the letter would dissuade her from visiting ZZL again.

Then he dutifully ordered the King which Leogrande had directed him to order yesterday, and carefully destroyed the telephone number Lorna Dune had left for notification when the snake arrived.

Now his day had begun. He had outwitted Lorna Dune. He felt elated, ready to handle anything.

His high ended three minutes later when a call to Alison elicited the information that Raoul was due in from Boston for the weekend.

If Shockproof wanted to, he could drop by for an hour after work on Monday.

6 *spaced out / coming down*

Beneath the gold Florentine faucets, Dr. Teregram was resting her head on the rolling pin which Shockproof had used as a float for her in the bathtub.

"I never knew that about snakes," said Alison.

"Sure. Most of them like to swim," he said.

"Finish this," she said, passing him the roach-holder containing the tiny butt of pot.

He took it, inhaled, and sniffed it up into his head.

Then another drag before he loosened the spent butt from
the holder and dropped it down the toilet.

"I feel good," Alison said.

"So do I."

"Do you feel super-happy, Sydney?"

"Ummm hmmm," he said. She was in white short
shorts with a white sleeveless shell, her black hair loose
and long. She was barefoot, sitting on the edge of the tub.

It was Monday night, the eve of Harold Skate's arrival.
Shockproof had come from work, after a depressed weekend of waiting for this night, fending off a series of calls
from Estelle Kelly, who would ring him up, ask him where
he was getting it, and then tell him to fuck off. M. E. Shepley Skate had gone to Bucks County for the weekend, staying at the Black Bass Inn near New Hope, where she was
investigating a bit player at the Bucks County Theater as a
possible principal in a new detergent commercial. Mike,
the NYU romance encyclopedia, had the garden to himself over the weekend; Albert had gone to a Schütz-
Palestrina music festival in New Hampshire.

Shockproof had spent a lot of time in the darkness of
his room, sitting on the window seat, overhearing Mike's
progress with a cherub-faced blond named Deborah.

— I didn't used to like the name Deborah.

— How come?

— I don't know, but I like it now.

— How come?

— When the person becomes dear, the name becomes
dear.

Much later he had heard them out in the garden again.

— I'd hoped for a simultaneous orgasm, Deb.

— That never happens first time out, Mike.

Shockproof had stayed indoors the whole weekend, wandering around, opening himself cans of Gebhardt's chili, eating it standing up, cold and from the can, wearing no clothes, reading books like *Memoirs of a Beatnik* from the Traveller's Companion series (*Serge had somehow managed to free his rigid member from his own shorts . . .*) and studying the glossary of terms in *The Drug Scene* by Donald B. Louria, M.D. (*bale: a pound of marijuana; blow a stick: to smoke a marijuana cigarette*).

Shockproof said, "Dr. Teregram is tired now. I'd better dry her off and put her back."

Alison squealed. *"I want to dry her off."*

"Okay." Shockproof pulled the King out of the tub and handed her to Alison.

Alison squealed again. "Drying off Dr. Teregram. Oh wow!" — and Shockproof realized she was receiving a thrill, imagining herself drying off her shrink.

Every time she was on the subject of her shrink, she blew her cool. She became foolish and unstrung, and Shockproof had to look the other way. She had told him she took the train twice a week to Philadelphia, where she saw Dr. Teregram at her home. Even her voice became adolescent when she mentioned her shrink, and her sentences were punctuated with squeals and giggles. He wanted to ask her if she had mentioned him to Dr. Teregram, but not so badly he could bear to hear she had not. The matter was left in doubt.

"Remember," he said, "always dry her off after a swim. She can catch cold very easily. And always put a float in the water with her, so she can rest when she's tired."

"I'll take good care of you, Dr. Teregram," Alison purred at the King.

"We should start adding vitamins to her diet, too."

"Sydney? Hey. I have an idea that would be super-sensational."

"What?"

"It's getting dark. Let's light candles and take Dr. Teregram in the living room, and I'll do a magic snake dance with her."

"Oh Jesus."

"What?"

"Nothing. Why do women always get it into their heads to dance around with snakes?"

"Not just women do it."

"I only know women who do it."

"Whole civilizations have done it. Haitians, Balinese, the Hopi, the Comanche Indians, everyone."

"She's tired now."

"What are you so uptight about?"

"Because she's tired, Alison."

While they walked back into the living room, Shockproof told her about Lorna Dune.

This got Alison laughing. She sat down on the thick carpet and held her stomach while she laughed, and then he laughed too, and realized they were finally stoned. He sat down beside her.

Dr. Teregram crawled in and out of their legs.

Alison and Shockproof laughed harder and threw their arms around one another, and he felt a sudden jolt when he smelled Y in her hair.

He stopped laughing and let go of her. She put her arms behind her and leaned on her palms, tossing her hair back and thrusting her breasts forward.

He had an erection. He pulled his knees up and hid it with his elbows.

He said, "That was from a good bale."

"What?"

"The pot."

"A good *bale*?" She laughed. "Where'd you get *that*?"

"Nothing," he said. "I just meant that was quite a stick we blew."

"You old 'head,' " she laughed. "Where'd you get *that* talk? You don't know what you're talking about, Sydney. Super-Sydney." She touched the back of his bare elbow with her long nails.

"I didn't used to like the name Alison." He led off with Mike's ploy.

"But now you do. Surprise, surprise."

"When the person becomes —" No. He sensed she was the wrong one to pull it on.

"When the person becomes what?"

"The hell," he said. "I have an erection."

"Fantastic! Let me see it."

He put his knees down and took his elbow away. "There," he said.

"I don't want to see it through your pants, Sydney."

"What are *you* going to do?"

"When? About what?"

"If I . . . I mean, I'm not going to just . . ."

"Oh *no.*"

"What's the matter?" he said, knowing how freaky he was being. Where was: *You were there when I was not. I was there when you were not. Don't love me, sweetheart, or I might stop loving you?*

"An eye for an eye, a tooth for a tooth. How gross," she said.

"I don't see what's gross about it."

"It's absurd. It's high school."

"Why don't we just go into the bedroom?" he said.

"The *bedroom?* That's really Establishment!"

"I know it is, " he said.

"Incredible!"

"I know it. Do you think I like it?"

Then she began to laugh. "Oh *no! What are we doing?*"

"Don't love me, sweetheart," he said gaily, "or I might stop loving you."

"Hey. What'd you say?" She smiled. "What'd you say?"

And Serge had somehow managed to free his rigid member from his own shorts.

"Oh wow, Sydney. Wow. Beautiful."

Without removing his trousers, he crawled closer to her

and sat facing her, with his legs around her, pushing his hands up under her sweater. No bra. Mind-blowing.

"Take my clothes off," she said, stroking his penis.

"It is true I told you I would love you, And I never did. But remember I'm forgetful, Little Fool," he said. He lifted her sweater over her head. He unbuttoned the side of her shorts. She lay back and let him pull them off her.

"Sydney?"

"Yes?"

"Where's Dr. Teregram?"

"Right. I'll put her in the cage first."

"No. Put her on me. Put her on me while you undress."

"Come here. Dr. Teregram."

"Watch her on me while you undress. Will you?"

"Yes."

"Oh, Sydney."

"Jesus."

"Look."

"I am."

"Look, Sydney."

"I'm looking."

"Hurry up, Sydney."

"I am."

"This is freaking me out, Sydney."

"There," Shockproof said. "There."

"Bye, bye for now, Dr. Teregram," she said, locking Shockproof in with her arms and legs.

Shockproof was mortified when he heard himself say, "Hello."

And her answer. "Hi."

Mike's clichés, he thought in the ascent, and crashing later couldn't care less.

It was after ten when they got around to eating everything they could find in the cupboards and refrigerator. Red caviar, salami, sour cream, Premium saltine crackers, Halvah, Creme Dania, Kraft Muenster, Light 'n Lively, and orange sherbet.

With effort Shockproof was keeping his mouth shut about what she had done with Raoul over the weekend, maintaining a natural *Promenade* cool.

"If I didn't have to get up so early tomorrow, I'd make you stay all night," she said.

"Why do you have to get up so early?"

"Shrinksville in Philadelphia. I have to get an 8:23 train."

"Do you tell her everything?"

"If it's pertinent."

"What does that mean?"

"If it's got something to do with what we're working on."

"What are you working on?"

"Right now?"

"Yes."

"My mother."

"How do you work on your mother?"

"Like she's really gross. She says everything that comes

to her head, and she calls me the Sphinx, because I *don't* say everything that comes to my head."

"I write everything that comes to my head."

"Everything?"

"I write a lot of letters. Not everything."

"Nobody says everything that comes to his head, but my mother."

"What does she say?"

"She says I'm the disease in the family."

"She says that?"

"She says my father's impotent because of me."

"What have you got to do with it?"

"She's always fighting with me, and then he sides with me because her temper's so bad, and he can't make love to her after."

"But aren't you away a lot?"

"Bryn Mawr has telephones and mail delivery."

"Are you the only child?"

"I have a younger brother. He has it easier, because they're taking a parents' effectiveness course now, and they're not so uptight around him."

"Why did your mother make you go to an analyst in the first place?"

"She read my diary. That really infuriated me; it was so gross."

"What was in it anyway?"

"Specifically what set her off was when she read about a foursy."

"A what?"

"A foursy. A double date. And then we all did it together," she said. "You see, my father's an oceanographer, and we usually spend summers in L.A. Everything's different in L.A. That's where I met Raoul."

"Was Raoul in the foursy?"

"He was my date for it. She made it into this big dirty orgy," Alison said. "We were all just swimming together in the nude. Everyone in L.A. swims in the nude. There're all these pools. You just do. You swim and smoke joints, and this one time it turned into a foursy. It was a lot cleaner than what goes on out in the bushes at their parties."

"But how come she still lets you date Raoul?"

"She said the whole thing was my fault. I wrote in my diary how I said we should all take our clothes off to swim, and she said I was the prime instigator."

"So she still likes Raoul."

"Sure. She loves Raoul. He's Harvard and he's going to be a doctor."

"Oh."

"She says I'll wreck Raoul's life."

"She really doesn't like you very much."

"It's mutual."

"I wouldn't know what that would be like," he said.

"Because your mother's neat."

"We get along."

"She doesn't have all these gross hang-ups."

"Not those particular ones."

"How'd we get on this subject? Now I'm down."

He reached for her.

"No," she said. "I'm coming down. I just want to be alone and go to bed."

"I'm going home anyway," Shockproof shrugged, "Promenading" it.

"Do me a favor?"

"What?"

"My car's parked on Irving Place in front of Pete's," she said. "It's a black Triumph convertible. Will you lock it for me, and then slip the key in my mailbox before you go home?"

He dressed and purposely didn't wash his hands when he splashed water across his face. He came out of the bathroom and found her sitting in the living room on the velvet love seat in a long pink cotton nightie, with the notebook labeled ORGANIC CHEMISTRY on her lap. She was holding a Pentel, vaguely listening to Brahms over WQXR.

"I just thought of something," he said.

"What?"

"Are you on the pill?"

"No."

"You're not on the pill?"

"I have an IUD."

"What's that?"

"Oh *no*."

"Never mind."

"It stands for intra-uterine device. It's a little plastic spring they stick in your womb."

"How does it work?"

Alison rolled her eyes to the ceiling. "Do you think you're going to like girls?"

"The hell with it then!"

"I just thought everyone *knew* about IUD's."

"Everyone doesn't go to Harvard and come down for flying fucks on weekends."

"Sydney, you sounded exactly like my mother just then. Your whole tone of voice. Your whole attitude. Moralistic. Disapproving."

"I don't care what you did over the weekend."

"Everyone's so super-possessive. It's incredible."

"I'm not," he said. "I'm *not*." Now it was all wrong, and not the way he wanted to leave things. This was an Estelle Kelly ending, the kind with bad feelings which would induce a giant attack of rejection diarrhea.

Alison said, "The way an IUD works is that it irritates the womb so badly that in trying to get rid of it, everything inside happens super-fast. The monthly egg passes through your system in a couple of hours, instead of a couple of days. . . . I'm sorry, Sydney. I'm in a bad mood."

"Skip it," he said.

"Hey. The evening was neat."

"Right," sticking to his policy of understatement. Then: "Listen. Alison. Remember." M. E. Shepley Skate style. "What you do with Raoul on weekends is your business. I'm not super-possessive."

7   *only the loving find love*

SCENE:	*Fancy restaurant. Woman instructing waiter.*
VOICE OVER:	*Why is Celeste Skinner McRee sending her salad back to the kitchen?*
CLOSE-UP, MISS MCREE:	*Because the lettuce wasn't crisp. You see, I'm choosy.*
CARTOON CHORUS OF GUM PACKAGES:	*Be Chew-zee, Chew-zee, Chew-zee. Be very, very Chew-zee: Chew-zee gum with flavor.*

"I don't see Raoul all that many weekends in the ninth place," she said. "His new schedule's a real grind."

Shockproof went down Irving Place spaced out from their good-night.

When he came to the black Triumph, he opened the door on the passenger side, got in, and leaned back against the leather to collect himself. On the seat was a flimsy square of violet chiffon scarf. He put it to his nose, smelled Y, then his fingers, and felt everything they had done on the living room floor zap back full force. He was going to have to lift something heavy when he got out of the Triumph.

Then he opened the glove compartment to see what more of her he could find. There was another square of chiffon inside, yellow, with a few things nestled in its center. He looked at them. Two were matchbooks. One from Elaine's Restaurant. One from Stay. In the ashtray was a cigarette butt. A Gauloise with a lipstick stain.

CANNON EXPLODING:　*Gun Gum!*

CLOSE-UP, MISS MCREE:　*You be choosy, too. Choose Gun Gum.*

Shockproof had intended to watch David Brinkley before he left to meet his father and stepmother, but the Gun Gum commercial hung him up, and he turned off the set and began brooding all over again.

When he had finally arrived home the night before, after walking around for hours, M. E. Shepley Skate had gone to bed. Shockproof had spent some time in the den looking through the record albums to see if there were any new purchases. At the start of things, it was M. E. Shepley Skate's habit to buy albums: a new Sinatra one, a new Peggy Lee or Lana Cantrell or Liza Minnelli or Jack Jones.

There were no new albums.

Shockproof had wandered back to his room. He had sat in the dark on the window seat listening to Borodin's Polovtsian Dances wafting up from the garden. Albert was back from New Hampshire, stretched out in the hammock, while a plump brunette with wild, tangled, hippy hair did needlework beside him in a director's chair.

Everything Alison's mother had said about Alison being the disease in the family, the prime instigator, and wrecking Raoul's life was being used to rationalize what Shockproof had learned from the contents of the yellow chiffon scarf. Long after Albert and Hippy Hair had left the garden, Shockproof was still going over it, following devious routes which led him to believe M. E. Shepley Skate could not conceivably be involved: that the souvenir from

Stay had been lifted by Alison during dinner at Elaine's. M.E. had not taken her to Stay; M.E. never took straights to Stay. Shockproof considered the fact that Dr. Teregram probably had no idea, either, that Alison was carrying on about her, naming a snake after her and drying it off, wanting to dance with it, and letting it crawl around her naked body. On and on. Bent.

Super-bent.

Sometime after Long John Nebel had concluded his all-night radio discussion of the 1965 World Bridge Championship Tournament in which U.S. players were accused of cheating, Shockproof had drifted off to sleep.

M. E. Shepley Skate still had the benefit of the doubt by the time Shockproof had awakened, but Shockproof had not had breakfast with her. He had slept through, pretending to sleep more than sleeping, entertaining half-waking dreams in which Alison was beating him at bridge by cheating, and Lorna Dune was dancing away with Erik Satie and Bela Bartok.

That evening a telegram arrived for M.E. She was working late, so Shockproof called the agency. "Well, open it and read it to me," she said. "I've got problems here Job wouldn't believe, and about two hours to solve them!"

He tore open the envelope and read the following: "Into the crowned knot of fire. And the fire and the rose are one. Found."

"*What?*"

"That's what it says."

"Run through that again, would you, Sydney? Slowly."

He read it again.

M. E. Shepley Skate sighed. "All right. Okay."

"What do you want me to do with it?" he said.

"Do with it? Leave it on the table."

"Why is it signed 'Found,' " he said. "Who did you find?"

"Why do owls hoot, Sydney? I haven't the foggiest, and I'm due downstairs twenty minutes ago. What time are you meeting your father?"

"Eight o'clock in front of the theater."

"Have fun," she said. "See that nobody rolls him or rapes her on their one night in the Big Apple."

After he had hung up, he had tried to call Estelle Kelly to make a date for the end of the evening, but her line was busy. He supposed he had lost her too, and he had thought of joining VISTA or the Peace Corps, channeling his energies into projects which would earn him self-respect. Now was the time to grow his hair, too, change his image, move out and find a crash pad in the East Village. Mainline. Beat his meat like Portnoy, find some maid to bugger like Mailer's hero, Stephen Rojack, pull a Henry Miller on Alison, hike over to Gramercy Park, tie her to the bedstead, gag her, and go for the razor strop. *On the way to the bathroom, he grabs a bottle of mustard from the kitchen. He comes back with the razor strop and belts the piss out of her.* Holding the bottle of mustard, or putting it down on the floor first? So the fantasy was arrested by a technicality, and Shockproof could not go back to it and rub the mustard into the raw welts. He was without a fantasy or any plan of action, which was his reasoning in turning on

David Brinkley. He hoped for a plane crash killing hundreds or the unexpected death of someone famous, preferably by suicide with murder second. . . . Then the Chewzee commercial. Now.

The phone was ringing.

Ann MacReynolds. Of the late great Ellie and Ann.

"How are you, Sydney?"

"Fine. How are you, Annie?"

"Oh, I'm fine. Did you have a good year at school?"

"Ummm hmmm."

"You're all graduated now, aren't you?"

As he answered her he pictured her: she looked somewhat like Sandy Dennis. Years ago when *The Fox* was *the* movie M. E. Shepley Skate & Company were all in a tizzy over — as Roger Wolfe might put it, "all in a tizzy over and twittering about" — they were all telling Annie, "My God, it was *you* up there on the big screen." Shockproof, the Fox, with his duffel bag swung over his shoulder, set down his duffel bag inside the barn, became Stephen Rojack who had just murdered his wife and now had Annie on her back.

"I have nothing in me," she said. "Do we go ahead?"

"Who knows?" I said. "Keep quiet."

And I could feel her beginning to come.

Ann MacReynolds said, "Sydney, the reason I'm calling is: Ellie isn't there by any chance?"

"No, she isn't."

"I see."

"My mother's working late."

"I see. . . . You wouldn't know where Ellie's staying?"

He weighed his answer. Rules which had always been clear before were clouding over in those few seconds.

"Sydney?"

"I'm sorry. I just dropped something. 1 was picking it up."

"Would you know where she's staying?" Ann MacReynolds, too, was breaking the rules now.

He followed. "I'd get hell."

"Sydney, this is important. I won't ever say you said anything. I promise. We'll forget this whole conversation."

"I drove her to the Algonquin with her suitcases."

"Sydney, you're an angel."

"I know it must be important."

"Oh yes, dear, it is. You see she had to have some privacy to work on a special project, and she forgot to tell me where she was. I have an important letter for her." Back on code.

"But don't say *I* said anything," he said.

"We didn't even talk, Sydney."

Shockproof decided to take his car, failing to remember until he was halfway to Times Square, that there was really only room for two. The thought of his stepmother stuffed into the trunk was his only gratification, until he saw a Western Union office on the same block where he parked the T-bird.

Shockproof knew what he was going to do, not how he was going to explain it.

He paid for the telegram and asked the Western Union girl to read back the message he was sending to Alison.

" 'Only the loving find love,' " she said. "And it's unsigned."

Instead of stuffing Rosemary Skate into the trunk, they stuffed her into the front seat, atop Shockproof's father, as they drove to the Orient Room up on East End Avenue in the Nineties.

"Are you sure they serve this late?" said Harold Skate.

"I'm sure," said Shockproof.

"Are you sure they serve both Chinese food and American?" said Rosemary Skate. "I don't eat Chinese food because of the monosodium glutamate."

"There's monosodium glutamate in everything," said Harold Skate.

"The Chinese are famous for it, though, Harold, and you know it. What about Chinese Restaurant Syndrome — headaches, dizziness, numbness and burning sensations?"

"Don't spoil it for Sydney and me," said Harold Skate. "If you don't want to eat Chinese food, you don't have to, but Sydney and I feel like some spareribs and some egg rolls and some egg foo young without hearing about Chinese Restaurant Syndrome, don't we, Sydney?"

"I eat Chinese food a lot," said Shockproof, "and it never bothers me."

"Is it nice American food?" said Rosemary Skate.

"It's very good," said Shockproof, "and there's a great view of the East River. It's the only Chinese restaurant in New York with a good view."

"I hope we're paying for the food and not the view," said Harold Skate.

"We'll be paying for both," said Rosemary Skate.

"As New York restaurants go, it's not expensive," Shockproof said, "and it's not crowded because not many people know about it." Shockproof had first gone there with Corita Carr and M. E. Shepley Skate at the start of things. At the end of things M. E. Shepley Skate was always accusing Corita Carr of sneaking off to the Orient Room to play footsie under the table with some new number, while they watched the river lights and mooned over each other. Once, Shockproof had taken Estelle Kelly there. She had made a face when she saw the room and affected a British accent, saying, "How veddy veddy romantic. I do believe I'll get good and pissed." Estelle Kelly lived in the neighborhood, which was the main reason Shockproof had chosen the Orient Room. He had decided to recoup his loss sometime after dinner, put Harold Skate and Rosemary into a taxi, and zap down and "jap" her.

"Not expensive by whose standards?" Rosemary Skate said. "This car is not cheap."

"Rosemary," said Harold Skate, forcing his patience, "Sydney's car is Sydney's business."

"This is a secondhand car," Shockproof said, as they turned onto the drive through Central Park.

"This is a Thunderbird nevertheless," said Rosemary Skate, "which in my book is not inexpensive. And not practical, but that's your business, Sydney."

"That's Sydney's business," said Harold Skate.

"I hear that park is filled with fairy boys," she said.

"Fairy boys wouldn't have the guts to enter this park after dark," said Harold Skate. "There's too many of your colored down here mugging people."

"There's both," Shockproof said.

"It takes all kinds," Harold Skate said, good-naturedly, "but I don't think the fairy boys want to meet up with your Harlem dope addicts."

"Why did we have to come this way?" Rosemary Skate said.

"We're perfectly safe," Shockproof said.

"If I knew you were going to come this way, I would have said something," she said.

"Rosemary, Sydney knows his way around this town. He knows what he's doing, don't you, son?"

"All the time," Shockproof answered.

Rosemary Skate said, "I don't think it's anything to kid about. In an expensive car like this, we're a target."

Harold Skate was a lean, balding redhead who wore rimless spectacles. When they had met outside the theater, Shockproof had to remind him that he was still wearing his Get Acquainted badge from the East Coast Swimming Pool Manufacturers Convention. It was a white badge with red and blue ribbons attached to it. Across the

face of the badge was printed: ECSPMC HELLO THERE,
I'M ————. Some convention members wrote "Bud" in the
blank space, or "Jack," "Fred," "Butch." Shockproof's father had written: "Harold E. Skate, Doylestown, Pa."

Rosemary Skate wore a corsage of red and white roses
with blue ribbons, distributed to the wives of the ECSPMC
members. She was short and round with good legs and a
pretty face, somewhat lost in plump width and blond
bangs. She wore Arpège perfume, which Liz Lear had
once declared no one but shopgirls wore anymore, and her
skirt was longer than any woman's they had thus far en-
countered. She had on a charm bracelet attached to which
was a miniature diving board, a miniature figure of a diving woman, a miniature figure of a diving man, a miniature circular pool, a miniature duck, a miniature lifesaver,
and a miniature float, all in gold.

After they were seated at a table near the window,
Rosemary Skate told Harold Skate to order her a Seven
and Seven, then excused herself to go to the Ladies.

Harold Skate said, "How are you, Sydney?"

"Fine."

"Everything okay?"

"Yes. Sure."

"Your summer's going along okay?"

"Yes."

Harold Skate frowned. He thought a moment. He said,
"Sydney, you respect your mother. Do you, Sydney?"

"Yes, sure."

"Yes, sure. Well, I don't want to do anything to change that."

"What are you getting at?" Shockproof said.

"Your mother raised you and I think she's done a good job."

"Then what's the matter?"

"Winters you were in school and summers you were in camp, or at the beach, but now you're older and this summer you're here in New York."

"I like it here."

"Your mother gives you a lot of freedom, a swanky car, etcetera."

"I'm seventeen. I'll be eighteen in December."

"Sydney, your stepmother and I think you should give some thought to the letter you wrote us some time ago, about coming to Doylestown and learning the business."

"What about college?"

"No one's discouraging the college idea. But you could start this summer to learn the business."

"The letter was a mistake," Shockproof said. "I don't want to learn the swimming pool business."

"One of our best friends is a veterinarian, Sydney. Dr. Morton Goldman. He's Jewish. Sydney, do you know the difference between what Goldy makes and what I make?"

"I don't even like swimming pools. I like the beach."

"We don't have beaches in Bucks County. That's why we sell so many pools. . . . The difference is about fifteen thousand a year, Sydney. And I'm not going to stand still at what I'm making now. Goldy has no choice. There are just so many dogs and cats in Bucks County, but we haven't even begun with the pools. And we'll expand. We'll go to New Jersey, New York — there's no top on our business."

"I don't want to be a vet, either," Shockproof said.

"That's what you'll learn to be at Cornell."

"That would only be part of it."

"If you lived with us, you could commute to Princeton. Sydney, I'm not pushing the pool business. Try it for a summer, and then go to Princeton. Study *anything*. I don't care what you want to be, but give the pool business a chance before you decide."

"I have a job," Shockproof said.

"They can always find someone else to clean out the cages at that pet shop," said Harold Skate. "If you work for me, you'll be calling on real people, people of substance who count for something. In one week, Sydney, I meet lawyers, doctors, your writers and actors, brokers, judges. I met James Michener only a few weeks ago, your author of *South Pacific*."

"Last week I met Lorna Dune," said Shockproof.

"Who?"

"No one," Shockproof said.

"Will you think about it, Sydney? The summer's just begun."

"I'll think about it."

"No one's pushing you," Harold Skate said, and then the waiter appeared.

Harold Skate said, "A Seven and Seven, a Manhattan with a cherry, and what would you like, Sydney?"

"Dewars and water," Shockproof said.

"Now wait a minute, waiter. Wait a minute, Sydney. Sydney, we're not going to break the law."

"I'm going to be eighteen in December."

"Sydney, this is June. The law is very clear on the drinking age."

"I'll have seven minus seven," Shockproof said.

"One Seven-Up and Seagrams Seven," said Harold Skate, "one Seven-Up, and one Manhattan with a cherry." Then he said to Shockproof, "In New York they're liable to put lemon peels in Manhattans unless you specify a cherry. . . . Does your mother allow you to drink, Sydney?"

"She treats me like an adult."

"Then she *does*," said Harold Skate, tight-lipped. "Well, that doesn't surprise me one little bit."

Rosemary Skate said, "What doesn't surprise you one little bit, Harold?" She eased her way in beside Shockproof. "It's a very clean rest room. That's a good sign in a restaurant. Clean rest room, clean kitchen. What doesn't surprise you, Harold?"

"The chickens are coming home to roost, that's all," said Harold Skate.

Midway through a third Seven-Up, Moo Goo Gai Pan, and Rosemary Skate's discourse concerning a recent "Ha-

waii Five-O" episode dealing with germ warfare, Shockproof saw Ellie Davies. She was sitting on a banquette in
the corner, with the river view behind her, facing someone
whose back was to him. Ellie was very definitely at the
start of things. She was leaning forward with her head
cocked to one side in a wistful way, smoking a cigarette
with her right hand, while her left hand played with the
silverware in front of the other woman. She was caressing
the spoons, which were about an inch from the other woman's hand, and smiling, talking in a very intense style.
They were not eating. There were cocktail glasses in front
of them, the menus untouched at the side of the table.

The other woman was a blond, but that was all he could
tell. He felt a glow of excitement at this serendipity, as
Rosemary Skate went on about germ warfare and the potential loss of Hawaii's sugar industry.

The other thing Shockproof was handling was a growing anticipation of "japping" Estelle Kelly, and somewhere
near the end of his Moo Goo Gai Pan, he ventured to put
in, "By the way, after this I have an appointment, so I
won't be driving you back to the Commodore, if that's all
right with you."

"An appointment?" Harold Skate looked at his watch.
"At this hour? It's almost eleven-thirty, Sydney."

"Someone I went to school with lives in this neighborhood," he said. "I promised I'd stop by and help him with
something."

"Help him with what at this hour?"

"His pet snake has mouth rot."

"Ick!" Rosemary Skate exclaimed, wiggling her shoulders and making a face.

"You know, Sydney, it's interesting," said Harold Skate. "A lot of people find snakes in their swimming pools. They fall in at night and drown."

"They don't drown. The chemicals in the water kill them."

"Is that so?"

"Do we have to talk about snakes when we're eating?" Rosemary Skate said.

"Does this classmate expect you at this late hour, Sydney?" said Harold Skate.

"He's a night owl."

Then as Ellie Davies was sending the waiter away from her table, she looked across and saw Shockproof. She hit her forehead with her palm in a dramatic gesture, then waved at him. Her face turned scarlet.

Next, the woman across from her turned around and looked at Shockproof. It was Gloria Roy, who lived with Liz Lear. Shockproof suddenly understood perfectly why no one from M. E. Shepley Skate & Company had met Ellie Davies's new amour, and why Ellie had not wanted Liz in on the onion pizza summit conference that night. Ellie Davies was running off with Gloria of Liz and Gloria! There was no predicting the turns romance could take among the ladies of M. E. & Co. Old friends suddenly felt new vibrations and the post office was busy with change-of address notices, the jewelers were engraving new sets of initials on cigarette lighters and the backs of bracelets, and everyone then settled in until the next turn of the roulette wheel. Shockproof felt like Florabelle Muir sitting on top of the biggest item since the Burton-Taylor shenanigans, back in the years when M.E. was with Cappy.

Gloria Roy glanced back at Shockproof and gave him a halfhearted salute, accompanied by a small, defeated smile.

With these exchanges completed, Shockproof saw Rosemary Skate look over at the two women, and then at Shockproof. Rosemary Skate's mouth was twisted in a tight little Pat Nixon smile.

"People you know, Sydney?" she said.

"Ummm hmmm."

Harold Skate was frowning down at his Chow Har Kew.

"Friends of your mother?" Rosemary Skate persisted.

"Yes, they're friends of ours," said Shockproof.

"I, myself, don't see a woman wearing pants to a restaurant," Rosemary Skate said.

Ellie was wearing a black velvet pants suit with a bright green signature scarf tossed over her shoulder.

Shockproof said, "They're in fashion."

"In *some* places," said Rosemary Skate. "Is this one of your mother's restaurants?"

"My mother doesn't have any restaurants. She's a casting director."

"Never mind, Rosemary," Harold Skate said.

"Women wear pants in New York all the time," Shockproof said.

"Which is another thing wrong with New York," Harold Skate said.

Rosemary Skate shot him a quick little smile of gratification.

Someone with a literary bent was in the fortune cookie business. Before Shockproof had opened his, he had decided the message would tell him whether or not to proceed with his plans to "jap" Estelle Kelly.

Shockproof's fortune read: "The devil will come, and Faustus must be damned."

Outside the Orient Room, the devil hailed a cab for the Harold Skates and went with his yellow furnace eyes, smelling of sulphur and tannis root. He envisioned her answering the door, half asleep. *Guy came in and began making love to her. . . . Bigger he was than always; painfully wonderfully big. He lay forward upon her, his other arm sliding under her back to hold her, his broad chest crushing her breasts. The hugeness kept driving in, the leather body banging itself against her again, and again and again.*

Now the devil was in the elevator of the building, ascending. Now sweeping down the hall, pressing the bell with his long, sharp nails.

"YOU!"

Shockproof stared up at Captain Kevin Kelly, towering over him in the doorway.

"Good evening, sir," but the Captain was crazily grabbing hold of his collar, eyes ablaze with some monumental rage. A whiff of whiskey worked through the punch of fear invading Shockproof's senses.

"You little bastard hippy! I'll pound the shit out of you!"

Behind him, "Kevin! Kevin!" — a woman's voice. "Easy, Kevin."

"It's the little creep in person!" the Captain said.

"Daddy?" Estelle Kelly's voice from the background.

"Shut up, baby. I'll handle this."

Shockproof was being pushed back out into the hall. The door closed on the woman's plea. "Don't hurt him, Kevin."

Now Shockproof was alone in the hall with the Captain.

"What —" Shockproof began, and felt a fist against his nose.

Next, Shockproof bent double with the assault to his liver.

"Mary Jane Marlboros, ah? You dirty little bastard!" the Captain bellowed.

At some point through tearing eyes, Shockproof caught a glimpse of Estelle Kelly hovering in the doorway, white and pinch faced. Then Shockproof tore free, ran clutching his broken parts, bleeding, hobbling, fleeing downstairs like a rat through the bowels of the building.

8   *my memory of it all is unspeakable*

The Skate house outside Doylestown, Pennsylvania, was a long white ranch house with a sauna in the basement and a swimming pool in the backyard.

Early that morning it was still dark when Shockproof had let himself in the window of the guest room. This had triggered the alarm system. A wailing siren had freaked out Daughter Skate, the Persian cat, who had overturned all the potted cacti in the picture window, then scaled the drapes, hissing, until Shockproof had managed to pull the siren's switch.

At ten o'clock that morning, he was awakened by Daughter's sandpaper tongue cleaning his swollen nose, and the sound of the telephone.

He planned to let the phone ring — Harold and Rosemary Skate were still at the Commodore in New York — but the ring was too persistent to ignore. He got off the living room couch and hobbled across to answer it, his whole body protesting the action.

"Hello?"

"Who the hell do you think you are, Sydney — Martin Luther?" M.E. said. "Why didn't you just leave the note inside, instead of attaching it to the door knocker?"

"I forgot my key. I was afraid if I slid it under the door, you'd walk over it without seeing it."

"Leogrande's furious, Sydney."

"Didn't you tell him I'd work tomorrow, my day off?"

"Didn't you ever hear of giving anyone advance notice? Now just *what* happened?"

"Nothing happened."

"Don't give me that. Estelle Kelly called me."

"Her old man beat the shit out of me."

"She told me. Are you all right?"

"No, I'm not all right."

"Did you go to a doctor?"

"I'm not a basket case, if that's what you mean."

"How do you know something's not broken?"

"I know."

"You're a damn fool, Sydney! What is this about mari-juana? Since when?"

"Since that well-known bent descendant of the Schiffs and Guggenheims and Kuhns, if you want to be gross about it."

"Don't pass the buck. *You* gave Estelle Kelly the pot."

"I left some pot there by mistake," said Shockproof. "She never touches drugs. She's a drunkard."

"Oh, she doesn't?"

"No."

"Her father got married, Sydney. Sunday night he brought his bride home to meet his daughter, and they found your little girlfriend sitting under a table in the living room smoking pot, with a loaded gun in her lap."

"That loaded gun's always been there in his sock drawer."

"Well, it was in her lap Sunday night, Sydney, and she threatened their lives."

"She might have done that anyway. She's got a father hang-up," Shockproof said. "I told you she had a father hang-up."

"She says the pot did something to her mind."

"Who told her to take the pot in the first place?"

"You left it there, Sydney."

"I *forgot* it. He *left* the gun there."

"He has a license for the gun. Do you have a license for the pot?"

"All right."

"I don't get you, Sydney. At all."

"I don't get you, either."

"What did you say?"

"Nothing."

"I heard it. What exactly don't you get, Sydney?"

"I get you. All right?"

"What did you go to Doylestown for?"

"I don't know. I just felt like getting away."

"Your father's still in New York, isn't he?"

"Yes."

"Then what the hell are you doing?"

"I'm taking a day off."

"You get yourself back to New York by dinner, or you can have the whole summer off, and spend it right where you are. Do you hear me?"

"I might spend it here, anyway."

"If you're not back in time for dinner, I'll forward your clothes."

"Did Estelle Kelly say *I* was responsible?"

"She didn't have to. You are."

"What about that well-known pusher from Gramercy Park South? She'll be some endorsement for chewing gum. Be Chew-zee. Drop acid."

"If you can't keep your head above water, don't go in over your head."

"Thanks for the advice."

"I told you she wasn't a little Stuart Hall girl, Sydney."

"I know what you told me."

"What's this about acid?"

"Nothing."

"Do you take LSD now?"

"No."

"Pot is one thing, acid's another."

"I don't *take* acid."

"Don't you *ever* give Estelle Kelly LSD, either."

"I won't be seeing Estelle Kelly."

"She feels very badly about it, Sydney. She was crying. She wanted to be sure you were all right."

"I may stay here and learn the swimming pool business."

"If you can take all that excitement, you do that."

"I wouldn't want to be responsible for anyone shooting Captain Kelly and his new bride."

"Dinner's at seven, Sydney," said M. E. Shepley Skate. "If you're not here I'll rent your room out."

"I may not be kidding, you know."

"I may not be, either, you know."

After Shockproof cleaned up the dirt from the rug and rearranged the pots of cacti, he went into the guest room which his father used for an auxiliary office.

Shockproof opened the file cabinet, M–S.

The folder labeled SKATE, SYDNEY (SON) took up most of the drawer.

Shockproof could not remember writing or receiving that many invoices from his father.

He pulled one out at random. It was written three years

ago, the summer he was at Fire Island Pines with his
mother and Corita Carr.

His father's part of the invoice read:

Dear Sydney,
I am sorry to be the bearer of bad tidings. Last week your
stepmother lost your new little prospective stepbrother in a
miscarriage. It would have been a boy. We are both very dis-
appointed. This is the third miscarriage as you may know.
But I have you to carry on the name, although we don't see a
great deal of you. It would be good for her morale if you sent
your stepmother a cheer-up card. Your stepmother and I were
very proud of your grades, and happy to know your mother
can afford a nice vacation at the beach for you, which you
richly deserve.
    Business is good, and I am the top salesman now. My
dream is to have my own business within two years.
    We are going to buy a house on Acquetong Road.

Affectionately,
Your father, Harold Skate

Shockproof's part of the invoice read:

Dear Dad,
Today I went clamming down at the bay. I have a good tan
and like it here. What I really wish I had is a mask, snorkel
and fins, so I could do some diving. The new wrap-around
mask costs $16.95, but a plain $4.95 will do. The snorkel sells
for $1.95. A good average price of flippers is about $10. I
could probably do the whole thing for $17. I don't know if
you'll want to add these vacation "extras" or not. The house
alone cost mother $3,000.

Affectionately,
Your son, Sydney Skate

No mention of Rosemary Skate's miscarriage; Shock-proof had never sent the cheer-up card, either.

Shockproof remembered that when the check for seven-teen dollars had arrived, M. E. Shepley Skate had forbid-den him to purchase the mask, snorkel and fins.

"If I say you're too young to skin dive, you're too young to skin dive, Sydney. How'd you con him out of the seven-teen dollars?"

"It was his idea I might like to try skin diving."

"Oh, sure. He wouldn't know the cost of a fishhook, and suddenly he knows the exact cost of a mask, snorkel and fins. Let me see the invoice he wrote with the check."

"I already sent it back, and I don't keep my copies."

"I told you not to play one against the other, Sydney."

"I didn't even mention you."

"If I know you," M. E. Shepley Skate had said, "you pulled your usual trick of exaggerating how much I was spending on you, to make him feel guilty."

So much for the story behind that invoice.

Shockproof's conscience hurt nearly as badly as his swollen nose.

Then Shockproof saw SHEPLEY, MARY ELLEN.

He removed this file and opened it to the first letter.

Dear Mary Ellen,
Make whatever arrangement you want and the sooner the better, for my memory of all of it is unspeakable. I am not going to fight you for the boy, since how would I care for a baby? You told me not too long ago you really wanted to try,

but I know better. The truth is you can't do what you want to do, even if that is what you want to do. You'll go back to your old ways. I told you once not too long ago, hang around with ducks and soon you waddle. You belittled the remark. Well, Mary Ellen, now you know the truth of an old saying.

I will never return to New York. I want a decent life somewhere among regular people. Just regular people — that's good enough for

Harold Skate

Stapled to the letter was a short note in M. E. Shepley Skate's handwriting.

Dear Hal,

Hal? That was news to Shockproof.

Dear Hal,
I'm so sorry. I am.
My arrangements will be very simple. A divorce. No strings. I want to accept full responsibility for Sydney. Naturally, anytime you want to see him — let's never put him in the middle of any disagreements we might have.

I'll pay for the divorce. My lawyer will always know where Sydney and I are, if you should want to see him.

M.E.

The next letter from M. E. Shepley Skate was a plea on her part for Harold Skate to see his son; detailed in the letter was the locking in by Shockproof of the various delivery boys and other tradesmen who called.

The letters which followed were mostly ones arranging for Shockproof to visit Harold Skate. Then there were letters from Harold Skate written two years ago, in which he insisted he wanted some share of the cost of Shockproof's education. These letters were more mellow in tone, mentioning Rosemary's miscarriages, and wistful with regard to Shockproof's future after college. Long descriptions of the swimming pool business and the advantages it offered a young man.

Shockproof was hung up on the phrase "my memory of it all is unspeakable." He put the folders back in the file, wandered around the house drinking Cokes, and mulled over the injustice of his never mentioning Rosemary Skate's miscarriage or sending some kind of card to cheer her up.

Shockproof sat down on the couch and allowed himself the security of reliving the hours in Alison's living room. He began handling that again, straddling her and being straddled by her, high on pot with Dr. Teregram slithering around them, chuckling to himself at the illusion he was just letting everything go up in smoke. . . . He was in a foursy. He was in a foursy with Raoul the other man. He was there with Raoul and Alison and M. E. Shepley Skate.

The hell. He took a shower. He brooded over what went on in a foursy. All four did what together? Would he have had to do it with Raoul in his fantasy foursy? There were classmates of Shockproof who used to take money from this rich swish VPS sophomore from Baltimore. He'd blow them for twenty dollars apiece. They called him "Two Tens" and made jokes about never bending over for the soap in the shower room when he was in there.

After Shockproof dressed, he wrote this note:

Dear Dad and Rosemary,
I came here for a while and in admiring Rosemary's plants
knocked them over by accident, but cleaned it up as best I
could. Rosemary, those cacti are really neat. This is a really
regular house. I thought you looked great the other night,
Rosemary, and I admire you, though I have never come right
out and said so. I will spend the summer in New York, since
I have the job, but will give serious thought to learning the
business one day. Thanks for the good time the other night.
Very affectionately, Sydney

Then he wadded the note up and shoved it into his
pocket. There would just be a hassle over why he had
come to Doylestown when they weren't there.

He took one last look around. He looked at his father's
bound copies of Effective Executive Sales Home Study
Course, the photograph of his father frowning as he cut
the ribbon outside Skate Pools, Inc., on opening day; at
the photograph Cappy had taken of Shockproof up on the
Cape the summer he was eight, wearing trunks, standing
in the surf arms akimbo with his head thrown back laughing (M.E. had been standing behind Cappy making
monster faces); and at his father's back issues of *The
Rotarian*, neatly assembled on the mosaic coffee table
Rosemary Skate had made herself.

He looked for some sign of this Hal who had, *must*
have, made it with M.E., under what bizarre circumstances he could not fathom. He found only Harold Skate.

Then he opened a can of Calo chicken parts for Daughter, dropped the empty can outside in the garbage, and
took off in his Thunderbird.

He drove back by way of New Hope.

On the main street there, as he was waiting for a light, he saw a sign over one of the stores.

M R.   B O R I S
Hair stylist for men and women

Shockproof looked for a parking space.

9 s. & m. yellow stella sweet banana paper

Mr. Jim, one of Mr. Boris's assistants, directed Shockproof to a top-floor apartment, three buildings away from the beauty shop.

The name under the bell was Loretta Wills.

Loretta Willensky answered the door wearing blue shorts and what looked like one of Mr. Boris's shirts. It was a wide-striped pink and white one, several sizes larger than Loretta. Her hair was long and blond. She was almost pretty, but she wore no makeup and her chin and forehead were broken out. She did not seem surprised to see Shockproof at all, and he remembered that about her: she was a very unstirred person. There was the story that once late at night years past on Fire Island Pines, when Loretta had been hurrying down to the bay to call her father to the telephone, she had slipped off the boardwalk and fallen into "the Chapel." This was a wooded spot for gang bangs, and Loretta had landed in the center of six naked men. Her only comment was said to have been, "Would any of you know Boris Willensky's whereabouts?"

"Sydney Skate. How are you? Come on in."

"I'm fine. You changed your name."

"I didn't change it. I shortened it," she said.

"What's this?" said Shockproof. "What are you set up for, a séance?"

There was a large circle of folding chairs in her living room.

"I'm having a sensitivity session here tonight."

"Is that something like group therapy?"

"Something like it. It's more free. Could you stay for it?"

"No. I have to be back."

"Your mother didn't tell me you'd come down for the weekend, too."

"I didn't come down with my mother. I came down last night."

"Your mother looks marvelous, Sydney. Some kind of a May-December thing, hmmm?"

"What?"

"There's quite a difference in their ages."

"———" What kind of a noise had he made? Something in between a word and a moan.

"If it's going to bother you, I'll get off the subject."

"Bother me?" Joel Schwartz had answered.

"It's best to just come to grips with it," Loretta said. "Once I came to grips with it, I lost a lot of my unconscious hostility."

Then she went into the small kitchen and opened the refrigerator. She said, "Jim came back from Philadelphia with some good shit last night. Shall we have a joint?"

"I never heard it called shit," he said.

"That's what Jim calls it," she said. She brought out the aluminum foil bag and the Yellow Stella Sweet Banana paper. "You're right, Sydney," she said, "I did change my name."

"You shortened it," he said.

"I changed it. I'm going to work on why I won't admit I changed it in my sensitivity session tonight."

"Where did you see my mother?" he said.

"Dad had a brunch Sunday at his place. She came with Liz Lear and Alison and Victor and Paul."

"The whole funny farm."

"I remember that summer at Fire Island Pines it bothered you to talk about it. Maybe you don't want to talk about it."

"I'd just as soon talk about it. What is there to talk about?"

"That summer I wanted to talk about it in the worse way. I'd just figured it all out, but you didn't want to talk about it."

"I'm sorry," Shockproof said. "I was a big letdown in every department that summer."

"The sex wasn't your fault," she said, lighting up. "I was very repressed. This is real strong gage. It may be hash."

"I didn't know what the hell I was doing that summer," Shockproof said, as she passed him the joint. "You were my first woman."

"I was repressing my own sexuality because of guilt over thinking of sex so much. You know how Dad always talks sexy."

Shockproof sucked up some drags and handed back the joint.

"What were they like together?" he said.

"Who?"

"My mother and Alison."

"Liz and your mother were competing over who'd light her cigarette sort of thing. She was like some sorority girl being rushed by the two of them."

"Was she staying with my mother and Liz?"

"I gather she surprised your mother by just showing up. She came in her own car."

"Surprise, surprise."

"She doesn't live with you, does she?"

"I don't know," Shockproof said. "I haven't been home in fourteen hours."

"Dad says your mother's finally turned down chicken lane."

"What's that supposed to mean?"

"That means she's beginning to dig young girls."

"Yeah," Shockproof said. "Right."

They passed the joint back and forth.

"Dad says you start off as chicken, and then you end up looking for chicken."

"I don't know," Shockproof said, "but this is good chicken shit." He had a real high appreciation of his own joke. Laughed a long time.

"It's good stuff," she said.

"I haven't eaten anything all day."

"Don't worry. I have all this food bought for my sensitivity session."

Then she said, "Sydney, do you know your mother doesn't know you know about her?"

"I know she doesn't know I know." Shockproof felt silly. The pot was there now and he was getting into a light, fuzzy high.

"She says a part of you might know. I heard her tell Dad that."

"That sounds like Mike," Shockproof said. "He rents our garden apartment. He's always telling girls a part of him really feels himself getting in very deep."

"Oh, I wonder what part *that* would be now," Loretta said.

"Were they hand-holding?"

"No. Long looks across the crowded room."

"Some en-chanted even-ning," Shockproof sang.

"You will see some chick-ken," sang Loretta.

They both sang, "You will see some chick-ken across the crowded room," and began to laugh.

"Were you ever in a foursy?" Shockproof asked.

"No. Were you?"

"Once when I was out in the Hamptons. They have all these swimming pools and everyone goes in nude," Shockproof said. "This one time it turned into a foursy. It was a lot cleaner than what goes on in the bushes at most suburban parties."

"Foursies and threesies are Dad's style. Not mine."

"You've grown up, Loretta."

"So have you."

"What kind of a life do you have down here with all your writers and actors?" Shockproof giggled and handed her the end of the joint.

"I'm not with a gay crowd unless I go over to Dad's. I have my own crowd."

Shockproof ran his fingers down the buttons of her shirt. "You look like a goddess," he said. He was remembering *The Magic Garden of Stanley Sweetheart*, when Stanley said that and smoked and made love with Andrea; then Andrea asked Stanley to look at her cunt while she masturbated, and say what he saw. Stanley tried to call it a vagina.

— *My cunt, she corrected him. Tell me what you see.*

— *Your cunt, said Stanley, I see your cunt.*

"You're very sweet, Sydney."

"Take off your shirt."

"You take it off."

"You take it off," Sydney said. "You have to want to take it off."

"I don't know about that."

"You have to ask my permission to take it off," Shockproof said.

"Oh I do, do I?"

"Yes. You have to say please may you take it off."

"Oh," she said.

"Please may I take off my shirt, Sydney, and show you my breasts," he said.

"A formal request. Oui?"

"It's not a joke, Loretta."

"You don't see me laughing."

"I don't hear you asking my permission, either."

"All right. May I take off my shirt and show you my breasts, Sydney?"

"Where's the 'please'?"

"Please."

"You may."

"Sydney, let's not make out in here. Can't we go in the other room?"

"We'll see whether or not we're going to make out at all," Sir Stephen told O.

"What do you mean?"

"First show me your breasts," Sir Stephen told O. "If they please me, then I might consider the rest."

O's face flushed.

It worked.

Shockproof was amazed. He thought it only worked in *The Story of O*. Loretta Willensky was a first-class O. The only flawed part was her back, which was spotted with pimples. Shockproof felt slightly asinine asking her to turn around slowly for inspection. With a back like that? The masterful Sir Stephen tolerating such a mess?

But he managed to say, "Very well. Ask permission now to show me the rest of yourself, Loretta. Name each part and remember to say please."

Afterward, he ate his way through most of the dips she had prepared for the sensitivity session. Loretta kept coming up to him and sticking her tongue in his ear, and wiggling his sore penis, and he wished she would put on her clothes, for even in some Greasy Louie's he had trouble maintaining an appetite if the waiter had so much as a wart on the inside of his index finger.

His nose hurt less now, and he no longer felt the other bruises from his bout with Captain Kelly.

"You know, Sydney, it figures," Loretta said.

"What figures?"

"Why you're so S. You have a lot of sadistic feelings toward women."

"That was a game we played. That was a joke," he said.

"Oh, nobody ever jokes, Sydney. You're S, and I'm M. I need strength because my father's so weak. And you're S to get even with all the women who took your mother away."

"Nobody took my mother away."

"You still can't admit that, can you?"

"Who took her away?"

"Come *on*, Sydney; women are your rivals."

"Why do you have to analyze getting laid, Loretta?"

"I analyze everything. . . . Have you ever been in love?"

"I might have been."

"I bet you haven't. I bet you're like me."

"Haven't you?"

"It doesn't seem real to me. I think I feel some emotion, but then I hear this little voice, Loretta Willensky's saying, 'Come on, Loretta. What kind of phony-baloney is this?'"

"Why is that?" he said.

"Why is *that*? Sydney, how many affairs of your mother's have you gone through?"

"I don't know," he said.

"Could you count them all?"

"I doubt that."

"I'd need a computer to do the arithmetic on Dad's affairs. Do you know how many times I've heard him say, 'This is the first time I ever felt this way about anyone'?"

"Does he talk about it with you?"

"Now he does. Before he used to say it to his friends, and I'd overhear it."

"How come he started discussing it with you?"

"When I was away at school last year I wrote him. I told

him I knew all about it, and I loved him just the same. Maybe even more — because after my mother skipped out, he could have put me up for adoption, or shipped me off to my grandparents. He made a lot of sacrifices to keep me with him. . . . I told him I thought we'd feel closer if we discussed it."

"Do you?"

"*Do* we! I've sort of assumed the parental role now and Dad's the adolescent. He tells me all his problems — how he's afraid he's going to lose Jim because he's getting older; the types he's attracted to; what he thinks of the fellows I date — everything. We really know each other now."

"What if he went after one of the fellows you date?"

"Oh, I'd give him a good race, Sydney."

Shockproof pulled his goggles down over his eyes and waited for the starting gun. He gave Loretta a farewell salute, and a two-fingered kiss, holding his fingers up in the peace sign. He was indebted to Loretta Willensky. He had looked her up while he was floundering, imagining she would be, too; they could flounder away a few hours together.

He had never expected to find a combination O, Mary Worth, and That Cosmopolitan Girl. (Last night I found Daddy making out with my date over at his pad. What Daddy does with boys is Daddy's business, but stay out of my territory, Pop! What's my territory? Any man I sleep with twice, or achieve a simultaneous orgasm with first time out, plus all the territory my favorite magazine covers. I guess you could say I'm That Cosmopolitan Girl!)

When Shockproof reached Princeton, he found a parking place, changed five dollars into coins, and stepped inside a phone booth.

"Hello?" Alison said.

"How's everything?"

"Who is this?"

"This is Sydney."

"That's who I thought it was."

"What's the matter?"

"What's the matter," she said in a flat tone.

"I'm calling from out of town."

"I know."

"I'm in Princeton. Just looking the school over. I might transfer here."

"Don't lie anymore," she said.

"I *am* in Princeton."

"You don't go to Cornell. You're just out of high school."

"I've been accepted at Cornell."

"You told me you went there. And you told Shep I drop acid. I haven't dropped acid in a year, Sydney. I don't even like acid; it ruins your chromosomes."

"You lied, too. About the weekend."

"I didn't lie."

"You said you were spending it with Raoul."

"Raoul canceled."

"I know. I heard all about it from Loretta Willensky."

"She doesn't know anything about Raoul."

"I heard how you spent the weekend."

"Sydney, I don't want to talk about it. I don't want to talk to you. Why did you tell Shep I take acid? Why did you send me that wire? That was really gross, reading my postcard and sending me that wire."

"Why did you send my mother a wire like the one Raoul sent you? That's gross, too."

"I suppose you told her."

"No."

"Why did you tell her I take acid? I haven't had any acid for a year. Why did you tell her that?"

"I don't know."

"Do you know the trouble you've caused?"

"What are you getting into with my mother? My mother's old enough to be your mother."

"Were you the one who told Ann where Ellie was staying?"

"My mother's old enough to be your mother."

"Ann was waiting in the Algonquin lobby last night when Ellie and Gloria arrived. There was a terrible scene, Sydney."

"I don't know anything about all that," Shockproof said. "What are you getting into? Do you know what you're getting into?"

"I'm not going to talk about it with you, Sydney."

"Ask your shrink what you're getting into."

"I just came back from my shrink."

"What does she think about what you're getting into?"

"I'm not getting into anything. I know what I'm getting into."

"*What?*"

"What?"

"I said what do you think you're getting into?"

The operator interrupted.

Shockproof stuck more quarters into the slot.

"I don't take acid, Sydney," Alison said.

"All right. I'll tell her it was a lie. Is that all you care about, what *she* thinks?"

"Sydney, I'm super-upset. I don't even think I'm going to my New School class tonight."

"You're handling too much."

"What?"

"You're going in too many directions."

"I'm not going anywhere. Thanks to you."

"Where do you want to go? Do you want to go with her?"

"Sydney, I'm not supposed to talk about this with you."

"Did she say that?"

"I don't want to talk about this."

"What did she say?"

"She said you told her I took acid."

"I said I'll tell her you don't take acid."

"Did you tell her about yesterday afternoon, Sydney?"

"No," Shockproof said. "She doesn't tell me things, and I don't tell her things."

"I'm not even going to get to do that gum commercial now."

"Is that what you want, to chew gum on television?"

"I need the money, Sydney."

"That isn't what you want. That isn't what you're getting into."

"Sydney, I'm going to hang up."

"Don't hang up."

"I don't have anything to say to you."

"My mother's going on forty-three, Alison."

"I'm going to hang up, Sydney."

"Don't."

"I don't want to talk about Shep."

"I'll come over when I get home."

"I don't want to see you, Sydney."

"I'll come by tomorrow on my lunch hour."

"Sydney, I don't want to see you."

"Then you can feed Dr. Teregram yourself. You can buy your own mice."

"Are they expensive?"

He slammed down the receiver, removed his racer's goggles, and pulled himself out of the race.

He had the usual longing to let Estelle Kelly drag him down the rest of the way, but he was afraid to call there.

He headed back to his T-bird, telling himself he would keep his promise to Loretta, and have her in for a lot of weekends. Massive doses of Vitamin A and pHisoHex soap had cured Joel Schwartz's acne — no problem — and one thing: Shockproof felt ready for a horny S summer.

10   *zippers in descent*

It was the beginning of the Fourth of July weekend.

Shockproof had gone back to his old ways, reading scores of novels, some books on herpetology, writing letters (never sending the ones he wrote to Alison), working overtime for Leogrande, and silently following the Ellie Davies–Gloria Roy affair. Liz Lear knew now; she was frantically calling M. E. Shepley Skate, crying one day, threatening to get revenge on them the next. Ellie and

Gloria had rented a cottage in Quogue for the summer; weekdays they stayed at the Algonquin.

During the past ten days, Alison Gray was never mentioned, but Shockproof watched what was taking place. There were dozens of matchbooks from Stay in M.E.'s pockets — M. E. Shepley Skate always went there a lot at the start of things, and there were long closed-door phone conferences with Cappy, who gave advice from Sneden's Landing, across the George Washington Bridge. Some nights M.E. pretended to be staying with Liz, because Liz was "having problems"; through it all packages were pouring in from T. Jones, Lord & Taylor, Bonwit's, Tapemeasure, and Saks — "the trousseau," Victor had remarked one evening when he'd called to take M.E. to theater, and spied the array in the foyer. New record albums included Shirley Bassey's, Eydie Gormé's, and Dionne Warwick's. M.E. had even changed perfumes, was wearing Cabouchard now.

Then that Thursday noon, the beginning of the long holiday weekend, as Shockproof was setting up a woodland terrarium for salamanders at the store, he heard Alison's voice behind him.

"What do you call this green snake?"

"Jake."

"No, but what's the name for it?"

"Green snake."

"That's the name?"

"Yes."

"How are you, Sydney?"

"Okay."

"Dr. Teregram's appetite is sluggish."

"You're probably feeding her too much."

"She hardly eats at all."

"She might want a change."

"Like what?"

"Probably other snakes. Something live."

"Oh no."

"Just drop them in and don't look."

"I guess you're super-angry at me."

"Why should I be?"

"It's even gross to think you'd admit it."

"I'd admit it."

"Are you glad to see me?"

"I'm not anything," Shockproof said. He had finished lining the bottom of the tank with gravel. Now he was pouring in a thick layer of sand and mixing it with humus. Alison was standing beside him, wearing white cotton bell-bottoms, a white blouse with the middle cut out, and a bright red and blue scarf around her long black hair. Y again, and Shockproof's stomach jumped at the scent.

"I'd like to feed Dr. Teregram before I go away for the weekend."

"Are you going to Quogue?" M.E. was going to Ellie's and Gloria's for the weekend, leaving tomorrow.

"Yes. I've never been to the Hamptons."

"I thought you'd be going there."

"Well, I was invited."

"Then go."

"I feel down."

"You look nice."

"*Nice,*" she said.

"Do you want some ribbon snakes for Dr. Teregram?"

"I don't think I can go through with it."

"Go through with what?"

"You know what."

"Then don't."

"Well, would *you* do it?"

"Go to Quogue?"

"*No!* I *have* to go to Quogue," she said impatiently. "Would you feed Dr. Teregram?"

"Oh."

"Well, why would you think I meant Quogue! I've been invited to Quogue," she said.

"I didn't know what you meant." He was standing there with his hands smeared with humus.

"I meant would you feed her?"

"I know what you meant now."

"Why would you think I meant Quogue?"

"I didn't know what you meant, that's all."

"Don't you get a lunch hour?"

"Yes," he said. "All *right,* Alison."

Dr. Teregram knew Alison, uncoiled at her touch, and wound herself around Alison's arm.

Alison had taught her a trick. She had stretched a

sturdy rope across the cage, and Dr. Teregram moved from one end to the other like a tightrope walker.

While Dr. Teregram dined on ribbon snakes, Alison said, "Look out here, Sydney."

He followed her out to the balcony. On a board resting in the sun, she had stretched out the molted skin Dr. Teregram had shed, and had painted it with shellac.

"That's why she wasn't hungry," he said. "But after they shed, they have good appetites."

"Do you want to turn on?"

"I can't. I have to finish that terrarium."

"Will it hurt to smoke?"

"I have to landscape it. It's all in miniature."

"I'm going to smoke," she said. "Do you want a sandwich?"

"I don't feel hungry."

She had some pot already rolled in blue paper. While she was lighting up, Shockproof noticed a suitcase and an airline bag near the door.

"All packed already," he said.

She went and sat down on the couch. "I'm being picked up around four."

"I thought my mother wasn't going until tomorrow morning?"

"I'm driving out with Fay Foote."

"End of succotash, beginning of pure corn."

"Smoke with me, Sydney, don't be so uptight."

"I can't smoke. A terrarium isn't easy to set up."

"What's this about the end of succotash?"

"Fay Foote calls being bi, succotash."

Alison giggled. "Hey. You know something?"

"What?"

"I actually think I shock Dr. Teregram."

"The snake or the analyst?"

"Oh, very funny," she said.

"I don't want one of these giggle sessions about your shrink," Shockproof said, sitting down on the couch. "You sound super-stupid when you're on that subject."

"I'm meeting everybody, Sydney."

"Who's everybody?"

Alison rattled off a list of celebrities from M. E. Shepley Skate & Company repertory: the fashion editor Cappy used to call "Round Heels"; the TV actress who played a lawyer's mistress in a series, and once set fire to Judy Ewen's apartment after Judy left her; the nightclub singer who years ago had tried to commit suicide by jumping off the Fire Island ferry. On and on. He could suddenly not remember one good thing about any of them; he was an American Legionnaire reacting to the names of hippies and crazies.

"Everyone's so interesting, I feel really gross around them," Alison was continuing. "I know I'm young and they don't care if I'm not anything yet, but the thing is at the rate I'm going, I don't think I'll ever *be* anything, Sydney."

"You're sure to be something," Shockproof said.

"I'm not creative, I'm really not," she said. "It's Bryn Mawr's fault. Of the Seven Sisters, we're second academically. Radcliffe's first. We're grinds. And I feel really super-seedy about the way I look. My whole clothes allowance for the last year was four hundred dollars. *Period!"*

"No one needs a big wardrobe on chicken lane."

She was not really listening to him. "Do you know Kay Grail, Sydney?"

"She used to burp me," Shockproof said. "She went with Gloria Roy before Liz did."

"I saw one of her movies when I was about seven, and I thought she was the most beautiful woman there could be, and she's still beautiful."

"Or else she went with Liz before Gloria did," he said.

"The other night she sat with us in Stay, and I couldn't believe it! Actually I've seen her in about ten movies. She doesn't look any older than thirty, Sydney. They all look so super-young and incredibly glamorous. I'm having such a fantastic time. It's all really blowing my mind, Sydney."

Then she covered her face with her hands. Tears were running through her fingers.

Shockproof looked at her. "Was that pot or hash?"

"It's me," she said. "I've been down all week. Hold me, Sydney."

Then she said, "Hold me harder. *Really* hold me. Sydney? I can really understand why mental patients need straitjackets. I need something to press around me, something to reassure me I'm not splitting, shattering."

"Well, what's Dr. Teregram doing? What's she doing?"

"I can't talk to anyone but you. I can't go anyplace without you. I don't feel right."

"Go anyplace? Where have we ever gone?"

"You know what I'm saying. I don't feel right without you. Lock me in with your arms and legs, Sydney."

She was pulling at his zipper. "Sydney?"

Shockproof had never made it with anyone without pot or booze. Even the first time with Loretta Willensky (whom Shockproof had invited for the weekend) he had gulped down four dark Löwenbraüs beforehand.

When he took off his clothes and saw his poor limp penis, he was convinced there would be no way for either of them to get it up. Not only was he sober, but she was crying, and Shockproof felt sorry for her. Pity put everything way out of whack, and when she knelt down and wanted to take his penis in her mouth, with tears still streaming down her cheeks, Shockproof felt like some bent fellow from the subways who had cornered a night nurse out at an early morning hour and forced her into fellatio.

Shockproof reached down and pulled her away from there. Then he got down there and began to lose the feeling he pitied her, as she made little whimpering sounds which were not sad anymore.

He zapped up hard as a brick, stood up and showed her.

That was when she started kissing him; they started kissing, long, deep, drinking-in kisses, and Shockproof was Charley of *The Pretenders* in the Warwick Hotel with Louise. He pushed her back on the couch, and remembered Charley slapping against Louise *like the waves of an ocean gone violent, and she felt the breaking of her own personal tide.*

Charley was thrusting and she was pulling and they were straining, and Shockproof soon stopped caring that Leogrande would probably fire him, and that Loretta Willensky would arrive to a locked and empty house. She was due between three-thirty and four. Shockproof had planned to unlock the back door during his lunch hour, as he had told her he would, buy a single rose from the Gramercy Florist, and put it in a vase in the den, where she was staying.

None of that mattered, nothing mattered now but Alison. They were wet everywhere and so was the velvet couch. She fell asleep first while she was under him and he was still in her, a deep sleep as though she had been awake for forty-eight hours, and Shockproof finally eased out of her, turned toward her on his side, and fell asleep too.

Her downstairs buzzer woke them up.

"Don't answer it," she said, hanging on to him.

"No."

"Oh, Sydney," she said. "Ummm."

"Alison? I love you." He remembered Rick saying that to Diane in *The Pretenders* and Diane saying back, *"And just what does that entail?"* He half expected the same sort of answer, or none at all.

"I love you, too," Alison said drowsily. *"Mucho mucho."*

Shockproof smiled. "Neat."

The buzzer sounded again.

"Sydney?"

"What?"

"It *couldn't* be four o'clock."

"Probably," he yawned. "That's probably Fay Foote leaning on the bell."

"Four o'clock!" She was up in an instant, flying across the room with her breasts flopping madly, making a lunge for the clock on the table.

"Oh, wow, this is really gross, Sydney. I'm going to keep her waiting."

"*What?*"

"I'm going to have to shout down to her," she said, scooting across to the intercom on the wall, "if she hasn't gone back to her car already. I'm super-upset, Sydney, are my white bell-bottoms all wrinkled?"

She was pressing the intercom button and yelling, "Fay? Fay? Fay?"

Shockproof watched her.

"Where are my panties? I can't wear these. God, they're wet. That's gross. Where are fresh panties?" — darting in and out of the room — "I can't wear these bell-bottoms. Sydney, you're no help. I knew she'd go back to her car, and now she's waiting. God. I'm glad we fed Dr. Teregram at least. Sydney, if you're not going to dress in a hurry, then leave a note for my cleaning woman I want her to defrost. Would you? This *is* gross. There. Panties."

Shockproof finally said, "I've probably lost my job."

"I can't think now, Sydney. It's better if you don't talk to me. I'm really super-confused. I can't find my Tampax and I'm going to get my period. Oh. I can get it out there. I can buy it out there. At least I packed. The hell with this hanger. Look at me carrying around this hanger."

She was dressed.

She was running back and forth searching for her makeup bag. "This *is* gross. I can't leave without it. I can't buy it all out there. That's too expensive. I know it's here but where? I can't lose something right in my own house."

The buzzer sounded again.

"Fay? I'll be down in a minute. I'm super-sorry!"

Shockproof sat up and covered his overworked and swollen penis with a pillow; it was Estelle Kelly's conditioning.

"That's mind-blowing!" she said to him, with a sudden smile.

"What?"

"You know where my makeup bag is?"

"No."

"I packed it! It's in the airline bag!" she said.

Then she blew him a kiss. "Happy Firecrackers, Sydney! Be sure the door locks behind you."

Shockproof called the number of the garden apartment. Albert was home. Shockproof asked him if he had seen Loretta Willensky.

Albert said, "Does she have very long black hair?"

"No. She's blond."

"Then I haven't seen her," said Albert. "Someone with long black hair was here this morning. She had a gift for your mother, so I let her into your place for a few minutes. That was okay, wasn't it?"

"What kind of a gift?"

"She didn't say. I let her in and waited for her. She called your mother 'Shep,' and said she wanted to leave her a small surprise. She was only inside for a few minutes."

"Since when does the general public have access to our house?"

"Sydney, she was awfully sincere."

"Oh, *right,*" said Shockproof.

Albert promised to keep an eye out for Loretta Willensky.

Then Shockproof called Leogrande and told him he had a bad case of diarrhea. From the rumblings in his stomach, Shockproof believed he was more of a prophet than a liar. Leogrande used it to elicit a promise from him to do all the night feedings over the holiday weekend. He told Shockproof the newly arrived red-backed salamanders intended for the terrarium had fungus. Shockproof was to give them individual potassium permanganate baths.

When Shockproof hung up, the rejection diarrhea sent him bent double into the bathroom. He was glad of the physical distress, glad he could not concentrate on what Albert had told him. He tried to think of what he was enduring in the bathroom as a total purge, cleansing him from all bodily and spiritual impurities, giving him a totally new start, as Albert claimed fasting was supposed to do.

He closed the balcony door to keep Dr. Teregram from a draft, and noticed there were no ribbon snakes left inside the cage. The King was coiled up contentedly in a corner, a bulge in her side, asleep.

As he passed the table, he saw ORGANIC CHEMISTRY, but did not open it. He looked at it and touched the cover. He thought of an afternoon at Fire Island Pines when he had come back to the cottage early, with a great haul of clams from the bay. He had rushed into the house. The door of M. E. Shepley Skate's and Corita Carr's bedroom was closed; the radio was turned up very loud. It was three o'clock. He had left the clams in the bucket, in the kitchen. On the way back to the bay, walking along the boardwalk, he had suddenly begun to cry. The tears came without warning, as though something he had eaten had been swiftly rejected by his stomach, and he had puked — then felt all right again. Once he reached the bay, it was over.

Next to ORGANIC CHEMISTRY was a piece of blue stationery with an A.A.G. monogram, and he was ready to dismiss that, too, but his eyes were too fast.

Dear Raoul,
Did I ever thank you for sending me Listen to the Warm? *Raoul, I can't talk to anyone but you. I don't feel right when I go anyplace without you. Raoul, I can really understand why mental patients need straitjackets. I need sanctuary, something to press around me, reassure me that I'm not splitting, shattering. Lock me in with your arms and legs. I am torn and bleeding inside, jumbled and upside down. And when, oh when will I heal? And what scars will remain?*

The letter was unfinished.

He tried to remember their exchange. I love you, Alison; so do I love you, Sydney. . . . Alison, I love you; I'm in love with you, too, Sydney.

What?

It was gone from his memory.

What was there was that corny cable which was the end of *The Love Machine. I need you.*

Only it was not signed "Robin."

It was signed "Alison."

It was not just one cable.

It was hundreds of cables and telegrams, thousands, all addressed to different people, all reading the same way, all signed "Alison."

Orchestrated by the tumultuous sound of countless pant suits' and trousers' zippers in descent.

11 a sensitivity session

"What was Doublemint trying to say with those idiot twins and double your pleasure?" M.E.'s voice from the den. "They were trying to say it's all right to chew gum *with* people. They were trying to say chew gum on a date; chew gum while you're walking, dancing, skiing, sailing, screwing. Chew! They were trying to make chewing gum socially acceptable! . . . Is that you, Sydney?"

"Yes."

"I brought Mr. Baird home for a conference, Sydney;

the air conditioning's on the blink at the agency. Loretta's here."

"Where?"

"She was down in the garden with Albert when I last saw her," said M.E. "And Estelle Kelly's been calling. . . . Don, what was Juicy Fruit trying to say? Stretch your coffee break: Juicy Fruit's flavor stretches. All right? Don, tell me what in the hell we're saying with this Chew-zee line?"

Baird, meekly: "We're giving gum snob appeal."

Shockproof proceeded down the hallway to his room, while M.E. let loose.

He went to the window of his room and looked down into the garden. Albert was playing Vivaldi softly, stuffing tobacco into the bowl of his pipe, listening to Loretta Willensky.

"I came away less afraid," she was saying. "I could relate to people. I didn't care whether I was Loretta Willensky or Loretta Wills. I knew I was me."

"You passed through an identity crisis," said Albert.

"Exactly."

"I've been to several marathons myself," said Albert. "They use many of the sensitivity techniques."

"Didn't you feel that you'd grown after each one, that you could *feel* more?"

"Particularly in the nonverbal exercises," said Albert.

"Then let's have one tonight, Albert."

"Mike and his girl would be all for it."

"Sydney will go along, too."

"How do you know?"

"He's very malleable. And he really needs help. Sydney should be in therapy."

"I could get this girl from the Women's Liberation Front, too."

"That makes six. That's enough people."

Shockproof sat down on the bed. He took off his shoes and socks, folded his arms, and examined the hairs on his wrists. He wondered if tincture of Merthiolate would be more effective against the salamanders' fungus than potassium permanganate. He thought of the way some salamanders lead a triple life, beginning in the water, later taking up residence on land, and finally homesick in advancing years, returning to the water where they were hatched. Alison was on her knees before him, with tears running from her eyes, but now he felt no pity for her and wanted her to blow him. He reached over on the table for the nail clipper and attacked the big toe on his right foot, remembering his own homesickness his first year away at school. It was a peculiar word, "homesick"; it could serve as its own antonym. The nail was curled over like a claw and he snapped it off, listening to the magistrate describe Camus's hero, Meursault, *The Stranger*, on trial for murder, as a *"taciturn, rather self-centered fellow."* The magistrate asked Meursault what he had to say to that. *"Well, I rarely have anything much to say. . . ."* ("A lot of the guys are actually homesick," Shockproof had written M.E., "probably because the food's so lousy.") Then during the trial Meursault wanted to speak out. *"It's a serious*

*matter for a man, being accused of murder. And I've
something really important to tell you!"*

*However, on second thought, I found I had nothing to
say.*

The shining surfaces of the guillotine severed Shockproof's head from his body.

Shockproof went across the hall to his mother's room.
He looked around for evidence of a present, looked in the
wastebasket to see if there were any gift wrapping in it.
He looked in the top two bureau drawers, then in the
closet. The room was neat as a pin. Happy, the maid, had
come to clean today instead of tomorrow. Tomorrow was
the Fourth, and every Fourth, Happy went on a church
picnic.

He remembered a long time ago when he was small, an
afternoon when Happy got bombed on Cappy's twelve-
year-old Scotch. "There just ain't no Cappy Rockefeller,"
Happy had guffawed, "but there happen to *be* a Happy
Rockefeller, and I is she." Cappy had fired her on the spot.
When M.E. had come home from the office, she had said
that Happy had been with her longer than any other
woman, and Cappy would go before Happy would. She
had gone over to Brooklyn to rehire Happy that night,
while Cappy moved in with Ellie and Ann. Phone calls,
arguments, tears, flowers; on and on. Sometime after
Cappy moved back, he had found a new gold bracelet in
his mother's bureau drawer with a gold triangle attached.
Engraved on its side was : *Happy, Cappy & Shep.*

Shockproof could find no evidence of a present. He

wandered back to his own room, peering down in the garden as he passed the window. Albert was pouring a beer for Loretta Willensky.

The phone rang twice. On the third ring, he picked it up just as M.E. picked it up.

Liz Lear: Shep?

M.E.: *Hello, love. dinner still on?*

Liz Lear: *Shep, where are you staying on the island?*

M.E.: *In Quogue.*

Liz Lear: *I call that real loyalty.*

M.E.: *I've been friendly with Elliot for years, Lew. You don't expect me to —*

Liz Lear: *I don't expect anything from my friends at this point! Fay Foote had them over for a barbecue Sunday night, now you're off for a weekend with them.*

M.E.: *I think we should recognize Communist China, too. It's a fact of life now, Lew. Elliot and Gloria exist — I didn't make it happen, or wish for it — but they're there.*

Liz Lear: *You could at least wait until the body's cold, Shep.*

M.E.: *It sounds pretty chilly right now.*

Liz Lear: *Have you talked to Annie? Talk to Annie if you want an estimate of the damage those two have done. She won't budge from Westport. She barely manages to feed the cat. She doesn't go out of the house; she's ignored all her appointments in the city. Ask Annie how she feels about recognizing Red China. And Ellie had the nerve to call her and say the cat would be happier in Quogue!*

M.E.: *Lew, may I call you back?*

Liz Lear: *Is Sydney sitting on top of you?*

M.E.:   *Business.*

Liz Lear: *Hurry, Shep. I'm getting into the Martins.*

M.E.:   *Can't you hold back until dinner?*

Liz Lear: *Shep, I'm a jet crash.*

M.E.:   *Lew, I'll call you right back.*

Liz Lear: *I hope Youth Explosion isn't joining us for dinner.*

M.E.:   *No. Alan's already left for the weekend.*

Liz Lear: *Good . . . She'll be a big hit out there. Gloria takes one look at under-thirty and runs for the wrinkle cream. Under-twenty ought to psych her out altogether. . . . Oh Lord, Shep, don't be too long getting here. Don't call. Just come and help pick up the pieces.*

He waited for M.E. to hang up. Then he put the phone's arm back in its cradle.

He thought of Mr. Boris saying over and over, "I never felt this way about anyone before." Was it better to feel that way a hundred times or never feel anything? Was it possible to feel without knowing you were feeling, to perceive at some later date that you *had* felt? Did you have to have intense feelings; would lukewarm ones carry you? He thought again of Camus: Meursault, on trial for killing a man, yet truly being prosecuted because he had not cried at his mother's funeral. *"Gentlemen of the Jury"* — the Prosecutor — *"I would have you note that on the next day after his mother's funeral, that man was visiting the swimming pool, starting a liaison with a girl, and going to see a comic film. That is all I wish to say."*

When Meursault assured his lawyer that he'd rather his

mother hadn't died, the lawyer had snapped back, *"That's not enough!"*

At VPS, Joel Schwartz had been one of the few Jews in the Episcopal school. Not a religious Jew; he called himself a delicatessen Jew. Yet he was required to attend the classes in religious instruction. Once they all had to memorize something about God. Straight-faced, Joel had quoted a verse from a poem called "Relijus": *Perhaps I ain't relijus, But when I say a prayer, I sort er feel inside er me, That God is always there.*

After that, Shockproof and Joel were always saying, "I sort er feel hungry," "I sort er feel horny," "I sort er feel like getting inside er some pussy."

Five minutes later when the phone rang again, Shockproof was still sitting listlessly on his bed. He let the phone ring. . . . A gift, Albert had said. What kind of a gift? How expensive? Alison was always complaining about her poverty, yet she had bought M.E. a gift. . . . Them that gives, gets. He had never given Alison anything but dead mice and ribbon snakes. Anything he could give her would be chintzy by comparison to the gifts M.E. could buy her. He never saved a cent he earned. It all went on gas and oil, rental library fees, paperback novels and books about animals. . . . Should he invent a new summer luxury and wheedle extra funds from Harold Skate?

"SYDNEY!"

"What?"

"Phone!" M.E. was shouting. "Telephone!" He picked up the receiver.

"Where does an old whore go to get laid when she's randy?"

"Hello, Estelle."

"I also called you up to tell you about my stepmother. I love *her* a *lot!*" she said. "She actually wears dress shields. Can you believe it?"

"How are you?" he said.

"Do you want a trick tonight?"

"How can you get out?"

"The lovebirds are off in Hawaii."

"Ha wa yah from Ha-wa-ii," Shockproof said.

"I could smash all her things. I could vomit in her undergarments."

"Where'd he meet her?"

"She looks like the bathroom monitor of a brothel."

"If it wasn't for her, he'd have killed me, Estelle."

"Sydney, I *had* to tell him where I got my stash. He held me down on the floor until I told him. Oh well, it was nice being under him for a while."

"He beat up on me, Estelle. He almost broke my nose. Don't I deserve any sympathy?"

"Yes, but I deserve more. She looks like a breast-pin saleswoman from Woolworth's."

"I'm sorry, Estelle."

"Sorry's not a cure for the hots."

"I think there's going to be a party here tonight."

"Is your mater having a bash?"

"Not my mater. Me, sort of."

"Are you having an orgy?"

"Group sex."

"How veddy veddy amusing. Am I invited?"

"Sure, Estelle."

"I'll bring my sleeping bag."

"There's this Loretta Willensky."

"There's what?"

"Nothing. Why don't you just come?"

"I'm already breathing hard."

"Just come whenever you feel like it."

"Oh! Oh! Oh! I'm sorry, Sydney — I couldn't wait for you."

There was a click and Shockproof hung up.

M. E. Shepley Skate was standing in the doorway. "Sydney, Mr. Baird is going to give me a ride uptown. I'll be at Liz's, love. I'll stay over. Loretta can have my room. I'll call you before I leave for the island."

"What are you pushing Loretta at me for?"

"Sydney, I wouldn't push that poor child anywhere near you. Why are you letting Albert entertain her?"

"I'm very malleable."

"Her father had me to brunch a few weekends ago. Try to return the hospitality. You *did* invite her for the weekend."

"I heard Alison Gray was at that lunch."

"Yes. Victor asked her."

She was smiling at Shockproof without batting an eye, a sudden bright smile with her eyes fixed right on his. He remembered all the times in the past he had seen that particular expression on her face: times she would say, "Miriam's going to stay overnight, Sydney"; "Sydney, Laurie's going with us for the weekend"; "I'm going to spend the night at Mitzi's, Sydney, and Liz will sit with you." There was the Christmas Eve when Cappy had moved out for good — that same smile on M.E.'s face, the same straight look into his eyes: "Love, help Cappy into a taxi with her bags," and when he had returned from doing it, the sound of muffled sobs from the bathroom, but M.E. had emerged dry-eyed and high-spirited: "I feel like having a hot buttered rum or two or twelve," saying nothing more about it.

There were occasions when the look drove Shockproof to overreact, to play some bent form of Let's Pretend with M.E., to say and do things to help M.E. believe that he believed, like some child going along with the Santa Claus routine, all the while knowing the cost of everything that was hidden up in the attic. At other times, he felt as he did at that moment, angry at the sham and the necessity for it, yet knowing no other way for them to proceed without it.

He watched his mother light a Gauloise with the thin gold Cartier lighter she had received last Valentine's Day from the woman who raised Yorkies, and liked to call him Sidsky, and M.E. Shepsky.

Bracelets clanked down M.E.'s arm; gold rings lined her fingers, all embossed with various sets of initials, and *Love, Forever, Always.* . . . Was she wearing something new he hadn't noticed, something delivered that morning?

"Why don't you go down to the garden and get Loretta up here and act like a proper host, Sydney?" she said.

He envisioned himself at Alison's, handing her a gift-wrapped jeweler's box containing a small gold snake pin, with room enough on its back for an engraving: *Alison, Sydney & Dr. T.*

He said, "I wish I had the money to take Loretta someplace elegant for dinner," intending to defrost Pfaelzer steaks from the freezer, "Someplace like the Sign of the Dove, Clos Norman, someplace like that," where dinner for two could easily add up to thirty dollars. He would never wheedle money for a summer luxury out of Harold Skate without moving to Doylestown for the summer.

"I wish you did, too, love," said M. E. Shepley Skate. "Maybe you'll learn to budget and manage that the next time. Kick the lending library habit, Sydney — you'll be a millionaire. Or learn speed-reading."

He sucked in his breath and shook his head slowly as he exhaled. "Stone," he said. "Solid stone from head to toe."

"Which reminds me," said his mother. "If I heard right and you *are* having a party here tonight, *don't* give Estelle Kelly any pot. I don't want her going home from here stoned."

Then she came over and put her arms around him. "Give your old Ma a kiss, ducks."

Shockproof smelled Cabouchard on her cheek and remembered Y. He thought of Cabouchard and Y intermingled.

On sight, Estelle Kelly and Loretta Willensky hated each other.

Mike and Albert agreed to charcoal broil the steaks on their grill in the garden, adding hamburgers and hot dogs for themselves, Deborah, the simultaneous orgasm philosopher, and a girl from the Women's Liberation Front named Maxine. She was the same plump brunette Shockproof had seen Albert with before, the one with the wild, tangled hippy hair who did needlework.

Estelle Kelly sat across the garden from Loretta beside Shockproof, drinking Rob Roys, and calling Loretta "Pimple Chin" under her breath.

Shockproof and Estelle Kelly were the only ones drinking Rob Roys.

Mike and Deborah were drinking Dubonnet and smoking joints, Albert and Maxine were drinking Sangria and smoking joints, and Loretta Willensky was remaining adamant about proving that she could maintain a natural high, as a result of her sensitivity session several weeks earlier.

Maxine had brought the boys a gift she had made herself, two tin pie plates painted in psychedelic colors, placed face-to-face with a mirror contained inside. She presented it after dinner, when everyone was high and listening to "Let It Bleed" by the Rolling Stones. Loretta Willensky remarked that it was a Ying-Yang benefaction and it turned her natural high into a crescendo.

"She's got more whiteheads than a cotton field at picking time," Estelle Kelly whispered to Shockproof. "I bet she pees purple."

"Shet yo mouf," Shockproof whispered back. "We is guests on de ole plantation."

"She's uglier than Grace Cottrell," said Estelle, "who happens to be the fuckface my father took for a bride. "

"She's not *ugly*," he said, a sense of fairness sallying forth from the maze of whiskey.

"If you put it in her, it'll turn the color of cow dung and smell worse."

"You're a gutter head, Estelle Kelly. A filth mouth."

"I bet they break the plates after she eats in a restaurant."

While everyone had gushed endlessly over the pie tins, there had been very few remarks about the costume Estelle Kelly was wearing. When Shockproof had answered the door, she was standing there carrying a flaming torch made of kerosene-soaked rags attached to a broomstick. She was wearing a red, white and blue plastic crown, a long white satin slip with an American flag over her shoulders, and white gym sneaks with red laces. She was carrying one of her father's chammy shoebags with a thermos of Rob Roys inside. "Give me your turds, your poor, your huddled messes, yearning to breathe," she had bellowed.

Each time a new person had arrived in the garden, Estelle Kelly had stood, raised her right hand, and shouted out the same greeting.

No one but Shockproof had known quite what to make of her. Loretta Willensky had remarked *sotto voce* to him that Estelle Kelly appeared disturbed to her.

He had answered. "Who isn't?"

"I mean dis-*turbed*."

Now Estelle Kelly was sitting in her crown and satin slip, minus the flag and torch and gym sneaks. The soles of her feet were covered with soot. "I think stingers would be appropriate now," she told Shockproof.

Loretta Willensky was arranging the chairs in a circle for the sensitivity session.

Shockproof went inside to make stingers for Estelle and himself, deciding that amongst these "heads," Estelle and he were anachronisms.

Albert had asked them all to think of themselves walking toward a wall, carrying an idea in their hands. On the other side of the wall was someone to whom they were giving their ideas. Everyone was free to enlarge on the fantasy. "It does not even have to be *you* walking to the wall," Albert had said. "It can be Brer Rabbit, Freud, Paul McCartney or Aleister Crowley — that's for you to decide."

"*Aleister Crowley?*" Estelle Kelly said.

"He was a mystic," Shockproof told her.

"Hell, Sydney, you can't sum up Crowley *that* simply," Albert said.

Mike said, "Never mind Crowley now, back to the game."

"It's not *exactly* a game," said Loretta Willensky.

Albert said, "You must tell us who is going toward the wall, what the idea is, how you get it across to the receiver, and who the receiver is. You must be honest. Tell your *first* fantasy."

"If you're honest," said Loretta Willensky, "it'll really pay off."

"What a challenge!" Estelle Kelly whispered to Shockproof in her Bette Davis "what a dump" imitation; then she crossed her eyes and stuck out her tongue as though she were gagging.

"Just go along with it," he said.

Shockproof was Atlas carrying the world in his hands instead of on his shoulders. On the other side of the wall was another giant carrying his own world. They met atop the wall, bowed politely, and exchanged worlds, but when Shockproof jumped back down and looked inside his palm, he saw that he had received a world which was all in pieces. The giant giggled and said, "I'm really supersorry, Sydney."

No.

Shockproof decided to carry the idea himself. Everyone in the garden was on the other side of the wall. He polevaulted over the wall skillfully and presented the idea for an orgy.

He chuckled to himself. He waited eagerly for his turn. The girls were going first. What did he care about a day of radiant colors with Loretta Willensky skipping through a wood of thick foliage — "Very sensual," Albert remarked

— an idea in her hands for some new unfathomable joy, utlilizing all the senses, shattering the wall with its wisdom? Albert could not contain himself and clapped before she'd even finished. What did Shockproof care that on the other side of the wall were people who had never received love? He had the real goods to deliver, the true let's-do-it-in-the-road message: a sevensy.

"No one can top that," said Maxine, flushed with admiration for Loretta.

Albert said, "As Kahlil Gibran once said, 'You give but little when you give of your possessions. It is when you give of yourself that you truly give.' Your honesty is beautiful, Loretta. That was really giving of yourself."

Mike began to analyze whether or not it was an idealized fantasy, while Deborah watched him with her wet lower lip hanging down hornily.

In a bored voice, Estelle Kelly said, "I feel a draft. Sydney, fetch me my flag." She was smoking her brown Nat Sherman cigarettes, alternating between matchbooks from Benihana of Tokyo, Ginger Man, and Luchow's.

Shockproof put her flag around her shoulders.

"I'd rather play elevator roulette anytime," she said.

"What's that?"

But Estelle Kelly could not answer. Maxine was into her fantasy: a lone woman walking naked to a barrier, handing across an idea to a world of men. "Love us," said Maxine, "for our natural hair, our eyes devoid of mascara and eye shadow; look and see our hands, our arms, our feet, and let the turning of my wrist be as exciting to you as the roundness of my breast . . ."

On and on.

Albert was nodding with understanding. Loretta Willensky was frowning with appreciation. Mike was surly-looking. Deborah's mouth was turned down in a grimace.

"We are *women!*" Maxine said. "Not chattel!"

"We are cattle," Estelle Kelly said. "Moooooooo."

"Shhhhh!" said Loretta Willensky.

When Maxine was done, Mike said, "We're philosophizing more than we're working on our hang-ups. This is a form of exhibitionism: we seem to be saying 'Look how beautiful our thoughts are,' instead of letting it all hang out."

"Perhaps you're threatened by the idea a woman has thoughts," said Albert.

"Let's go on, anyway," Loretta Willensky said. "We'll just have a general discussion after each fantasy is presented. We'll brainstorm after the whole group has participated. . . . Estelle?"

"You're on the other side of the wall, Loretta," said Estelle Kelly, "and my idea is for you to go fuck yourself."

A useless whimper escaped from somewhere inside Shockproof, then silence in the garden, and Albert's subsequent invitation to Loretta Willensky, Mike, and Deborah, for coffee inside.

Shockproof had never made out with anyone with such dirty feet. He was Barney on the road with Siam Miami, who never took baths and had a habit of farting. He was crocked and deep into that book while he laid Estelle in his bedroom. Estelle was Siam Miami whose raw and touching singing gave listeners the unguarded sex they dreamed about; her knish-warmer of a smile, her natural sex appeal, her ambitious drive can't protect her from her vulnerable honesty.

He was headlong into their third go-around when Estelle said, "No more, no more, I came!"

Estelle slipped from 69 to 99. "Where's my grog, mate?"

"On the table beside you," Shockproof said. He rolled away from her and wiped his wet face with his wet fingers.

"Slippery deck tonight, sailor," said Estelle, reaching for her stinger.

"What's elevator roulette?" he asked.

"You have to be in a big modern apartment building with piles of elevators."

"Go on."

"You strip, and whoever's with you strips. You all get into separate elevators on the top floor. It's best to play it around one or two in the morning, when there's less traffic in the elevators. The first one who meets anyone going up or down wins five bucks from the others."

"Did you ever win?"

"Once."

"What happened."

"I got on at the twenty-second floor, and a lady got on at

the eleventh. We were going down. She was walking her
Yorkie."

"What'd you *say*?"

"I was way over in the corner. She didn't see me until
the door closed. She looked at me and then looked away
fast. I said, 'Support Mental Health.' "

"What'd she do?"

"She just watched the floor indicator like it was a Geiger
counter and the building was radioactive. Then when we
got to the lobby, she picked up the dog and ran. . . . I
won fifteen dollars."

Shockproof closed his eyes to see if everything was going around. He opened them. "Sex sobers you up," he said.

The mood down in the garden had become more solemn. He listened for a few seconds to Bach's Mass in B
minor.

"She really pisses me off," Estelle Kelly said.

"Did you see the look on her face after you told her to go
fuck herself?"

"I don't mean the pimple chin. I mean Grace Cottrell.
Gracious Me."

"You'll be going back to school soon," he said.

"That's what you think. . . . Don't play with my tits.
Sex is over."

"Jesus," Shockproof complained.

"They're not letting me go back for my senior year. Gracious Me thinks I need a home life."

"The Captain better get his gun out of that sock
drawer."

"He turned in his gun. Gracious Me has made him a real Goody Two Shoes. We don't even have a cocktail hour anymore when he's home. I can't get anything stronger than Dr. Pepper around that place anymore."

"I'm sorry, Stel."

"*Es*-stelle."

"You've gone to that school since you were twelve. You ought to be able to graduate.with your class."

"Gracious Me makes Mrs. *Portnoy* look like an indifferent parent."

He thought of Portnoy and Monkey picking up Lina, the whore, on the Via Veneto for a triumvirate. His blood was coming back in circulation.

"Gracious Me has cut off his balls," said Estelle.

"He had all his balls the night he lit into me."

" 'Estelle,' says she, 'how would you like your room redecorated, dear, would you like that, dear? Wouldn't it be fun to re-decorate your room together?' I'd like to re-decorate her twat."

"Does she know how much you hate her?"

" 'Estelle,' she says, 'I *know* no one can take your *real* mother's place. I'm not going to try to take your real mother's place.' I said, 'Be my guest; there's plenty of room in the cemetery.' "

Just as he was planning another mild assault on her, he perceived the fact Estelle Kelly was crying. He weighed the notion of putting his arms around her for sheer comfort, while he remembered the time Corita Carr had moved in. "Do you like ball games?" she had asked, punching his shoulder. "*I* like ball games. We'll be tooling off to Shea and Yankee every chance we get, Syd."

"In another year you'll go to college, anyway," he said softly, trying to pretend to her he didn't know she was crying.

"Sure," her voice cracked. "Hunter. Barnard. I'll have my pick. As long as it's in New York near Gracious Me and Balls Off. Oh, I know her, Sydney. She's going to have me on a dog lead. I'll be sleeping in a birdcage. The only way I got out this weekend was by telling them I was visiting Agatha Henry in Larchmont. They would have dragged me to Hawaii."

Shockproof put his hand in hers. "Aloha," he said.

She shook her hand away from his impatiently. "No shitty pity."

He said, "Listen. Estelle. You're going to be eighteen in the fall, aren't you?"

"So what?" she sniffled.

"I'm going to be eighteen, too."

"So what, so what, so what?"

"*Siam, there is nothing I want to do more in this world than marry you.*"

"*Thank God for my hot crotch.*"

"*I'm not marrying you for your hot crotch.*"

"Nothing," Shockproof said. "We could get married."

"Piss off."

"We could."

"Piss off, Sydney Skate. Why would you marry me?"

"There is nothing I want to do more in this world than marry you," Barney said.

"Oh, fuck, do you think I'm swallowing that one?"

"Listen. Stel. I —"

"*Es*-stelle!"

"Estelle."

"You *what?*"

"I'd marry you."

"Why?"

"To get you away from Gracious Me and Balls Off."

"You *would?*" She sat up in bed. "You would? Not because you loved me," she said threateningly.

"No. I wouldn't marry you for that."

"Are you sure?"

"I said why I'd marry you."

"Boy, that would make them shit chocolate ice cream."

"You'd have to do something about the way you express yourself."

"Anything. I'd do anything. I'd kiss Loretta Willensky's ass."

"I don't know if you *can* do anything about the way you express yourself," he said.

"Yes, I can. I can change."

"Would you be willing to live in Ithaca, New York?"

"I'd live in a sewer."

"I have to go to Cornell. You'd have to get a job in Ithaca."

"I can type. I can wait table. I'm as strong as an ox. Feel my muscle."

"I believe you."

"*Feel* it." She put down her stinger and raised her arm in a fist.

"Super-strong," he said.

"Sydney?"

"What?"

"Do something really foul to me fast. I don't want to get my hopes up."

In the early morning, Shockproof woke up to see the American flag moving across his bedroom. Estelle bent over to tie her gym sneaks.

His head was throbbing with pain. He held it between his hands as he sat up.

"Estelle? What are you doing?"

"What does it look like I'm doing?"

"Why are you leaving?"

She didn't answer. Shockproof eased himself out of bed. He had crashed into a horrendous hangover. His whole being was churning with insecurity and need and the hangover hots. He made his way slowly across to her with an erection.

"Put something around you!" she snapped.

"Please" was all he could manage to say. He could no more have made out with her than he could have found the energy to gargle, but he wanted her there. He didn't want to be left now in this shattered condition.

"I can't find my change purse, or I'd have been out of here ten minutes ago!" she said.

"No. Don't."

"I need my purse for cab fare."

"Why are you leaving, Stel? *Estelle?*"

"Don't walk around like that!"

"I could walk out on Nineteenth Street like this and get less attention than you'll get in that outfit at this hour!"

"Lend me cab fare. My purse is in the garden."

"I wasn't putting you on about marrying you."

"Lend me cab fare."

"What's this thing you have about the morning after?"

"It's a thing I have about the morning after," she said, grabbing his wallet from his desk. "I'm taking three dollars. I'll pay you back."

"You can't go out in a satin slip with the flag over your shoulder."

"It's the Fourth of July."

"Don't you want some juice first?"

"I had some juice. I was juiced last night."

"I'll put some clothes on and help you get a taxi."

"Mind your own business, Buster. There's only room for one in this cockpit."

She went across and opened the bedroom door.

"Don't," Shockproof said.

Estelle Kelly didn't answer.

The front door slammed.

Shockproof was standing there holding his head when his mother's bedroom door opened.

Loretta Willensky came across the hall carrying a book. She was wearing a thin white mini-nightie.

"Is she gone, Sydney?"

"Yes," Shockproof said, "I'm sorry," reaching for his shirt to put around him.

As she came into the bedroom, he fastened the shirt around his waist and backed up to the bed. He sat down. "I'm really sorry," he said. "Things got out of hand."

"I'm the one who's sorry, Sydney. I didn't sleep all night."

"Why?"

She was carrying *Listen to the Warm* by Rod McKuen. There was a paperclip attaching a sheet of familiar blue stationery to the front cover, but Shockproof recognized the jacket from seeing the book at Alison's. He saw Alison's handwriting across the stationery.

"I had no idea how you felt, Sydney." Loretta sat down beside him.

"About what, Loretta?"

She put the book on her lap and Shockproof began to make out the writing on the stationery. It was set up like a poem. *I can understand why mental patients,/ Need straitjackets.*

"What a sweet thing to do," said Loretta Willensky, "to leave a present under my pillow."

> *They need sanctuary; you be*
> *Mine.*
> *I want you to press around me, hold me,*
> *Reassure me that I'm not splitting,*
> *Shattering.*
> *I am torn and bleeding inside,*
> *Jumbled and upside down.*

For a moment Shockproof couldn't get it together. Then he remembered Victor's mentioning that Alison had dropped off a gift for M.E.

"I'm very moved, Sydney," Loretta said. "I want to think hard about it before we discuss it."

"That's perfectly understandable," he said.

He stared wearily at the blue stationery.

"Please forgive me, Sydney," said Loretta.

> *Please stay close. I can't*
> *Talk to anyone but you, I don't*
> *Feel right when you aren't*
> *Close.*

"How ironic that I'd turn the evening into a sensitivity session," Loretta said, "when I was so insensitive myself. I didn't even come up from the garden when I knew you were home. I thought you'd pawned me off on Albert."

"Well," Shockproof said.

"No wonder you tried to get back at me with that *creature.*"

"Estelle," he said.

"Yes. That Estelle. Sydney, I didn't sleep all night."

"I didn't get much sleep, either."

"Sydney?"

"What?"

"Can we just lie down together and hold each other?"

"Lie down?"

"Don't be afraid," said Loretta Willensky, taking his hand, pulling him down beside her. "You've taken a big step, Sydney."

"I have?"

"You've reached out. I didn't think you were capable of it."

"Oh," he said.

"Sydney, remember something tomorrow: what you did today was very brave, regardless of its outcome. You committed yourself. Will you remember that?"

"Sure. Yes. I'll remember."

She put her arms around him. "Don't try to talk now," she said. "We're just going to hold each other."

His hangover made him helpless against the suggestion. He thought of Estelle Kelly out on Third Avenue somewhere in her flag, trying to hail a taxi. Then he shut his eyes, trying not to believe he could contract acne cheek to cheek.

"Relax," Loretta Willensky said. "Aim for a nonverbal closeness."

12 *the fear and the trembling and the hangover hots*

Shockproof had showered, shaved, splashed Aramis across his neck, and dressed, but it did nothing to improve his physical and mental condition. He was suffering from hangover hots in the acute phase, along with hangover anxiety.

Loretta Willensky was still wearing her thin white mini-nightie.

She was sitting across from him over a breakfast of

bacon and eggs which she had fixed, affecting a thoughtful expression tinged with sadness.

"Someone once wrote," she began, sounding like Albert with one of his borrowed authority ploys from *Bartlett's Quotations,* " 'If equal affection cannot be, let the more loving one be me." Did you ever come across that in all your readings, Sydney?"

"No," he said. His knee was inching toward her knee under the kitchen table. He gulped down a glass of ice water to try and quench the hangover thirst.

"Whoever wrote that," she said, "understood that *you're* really the more fortunate of the two of us."

He wanted to get past all this mishmash of analysis and revelation.

"Whoever wrote the copy on the Bromo-Seltzer label understood me," he chuckled.

"Oh, Sydney, Sydney, try to communicate with me."

"I'm trying, Loretta, but I don't feel very well this noon."

"That's why I dislike drinkers. Why can't you stick to shit, Sydney?"

"That's probably what I'll do," he said.

"You don't want to try and communicate, do you? You never have wanted to, have you, not in an open confrontation?"

"Yes. Sure."

"No, Sydney. Right now you're trying to play kneesy under the table, and whoever it is who asked me for sanctuary in a very *dear* poem, which really, really moved me,

Sydney, is unwilling to plain and simple communicate with me."

"When I write I get carried away sometimes," he said.

"Don't apologize. Don't be defensive."

"Poetry is like fantasy, Loretta."

"Never mind that. You reached out."

"Poets get carried away with words."

"Anyone, Sydney, *anyone* who can show me his vulnerability has my deep affection."

"It doesn't necessarily mean the poem *means* anything."

"But when two people need sanctuary, they can't find it with each other."

"You might write the same poem to ten people," he said. "That's the way certain poets are."

"You see, I need sanctuary too, Sydney. That's what I'm trying to communicate to you."

Morton Earbrow was telling Gillian his knees and elbows were wet, he'd soil her couch, as *Naked Came the Stranger. Yes, by God, communicate with someone.*

"Sydney," Loretta Willensky said, "I can't give you sanctuary."

"That's okay, Loretta." Should he be Sir Stephen again and order O to put down the marmalade jar and lift up her mini-nightie?

"Sydney, I think something happened between Albert and me."

"Can't you remember? Did you black out or something?"

"Sydney, please *listen! I* wasn't drinking last night. I

was maintaining a natural high. I don't mean something physical."

"I get it."

"Can you understand why, Sydney?"

"Sure. I understand." He ran his fingers along her arm.

Loretta Willensky looked down at his fingers but did not move her arm.

"Because of our backgrounds, Sydney," she said, "you and I both need very special people."

"Right."

"People who'll sense we've been traumatized."

"I like Albert. I think he's fine." Shockproof was thinking of doing something freaky with the marmalade and her breasts.

"Sydney, I'm not sure you're even capable of communicating." She pulled her arm from his reach.

"Yes I am." He gulped down another glass of water.

"I didn't sleep very much and it's hard, but I want to try and get across my true feelings about your gift."

"It was a very lousy poem, Loretta. I don't want you to think that's any sample of my poetry."

"Sydney, it was a very moving poem."

"I can certainly do better."

"And I'm really very fond of you, Sydney."

"I am of you, too, Loretta."

"And I *enjoyed* that afternoon you came to my apartment."

"Oh I did, too, Loretta."

"I *did*."

"I did, too."

Morton Earbrow was communicating in the cool darkness with Gillian.

"Sydney?"

"What?"

Faster and faster they communicated, harder and harder, in dozens of places, in countless ways. Fingers and nails on skin, their great shudders of total communication. There were explosions of understandings and —

"Sydney! What are you doing with the marmalade?"

"Put your nipples out, Loretta, and say please. The marmalade's for your nipples."

Loretta Willensky slapped her fork to the plate. "I'm *in love* with Albert, Sydney!"

"Okay, but —" was lost in the scraping noise of her chair being pushed away from the table.

"I *wanted* to break it gently!"

Loretta Willensky fled from the kitchen, as he licked the marmalade off his fingers.

At Zappy Zoo Land that afternoon, there was a postcard on Leogrande's desk, next to a note from Leogrande.

The postcard had been mailed from Lightning Strikes, a nightclub on Third Street in Greenwich Village.

Working here now and need snakes if you no longer handel please advize where a place does and call anytime eves after nine untill two morn. Leave message if working will return call regards your old custemer, Lorna Dune.

Leogrande's note read:

Sydney, This unannounced beforehand time off must stop,
or I'll can you. Call Miss Dune and tell her we can stock her.
Dismantle the aquatic terrarium after treating the salaman-
ders and sterilize the tank with disinfectant. You'll have to
force-feed the new python, also check for mites. All our ship-
ments from Dutton Animal Farm have been defective lately.
Hate to cut off Cal Dutton, but that's the next step unless I go
down and take a look and talk with Cal myself. Check all his
shipments very carefully from now on. Leo.

Shockproof didn't get home until five o'clock.

Loretta Willensky was down in the garden with Albert.
They were listening to Julian Bream and George Malcolm
play Bach sonatas. Shockproof did not want to watch or
hear them. He shut the window of his bedroom and
turned on the air conditioner. Then he dialed Estelle
Kelly's number.

"Good-bye," she said.

"How did you know it was me?" he said.

"You're the only one it could be."

"We could go for a walk, Stel. Estelle."

"No we couldn't."

"I'd come up and we could walk over to Carl Schurz
Park."

"No more shitty pity," she said.

"That's not why I'm suggesting it."

"You'd marry the Easter Seal girl if she was old
enough."

"It hasn't got anything to do with pity for you. I'm just
down."

"Well, I'm on my way up."

"Are you having a drink?"

"No. Up up and away. Fly the friendly skies of United."

"What are you talking about?"

"I'm going to Hawaii," she said. "In one hour."

"*Why?*"

"My place eez vit dem," she said, trying a Maria Ouspenskaya imitation gleaned from an old TV movie, "and I vill go to dem."

"You *hate* Gracious Me!"

"I'm declaring a moratorium," she said. "Anyway, certain people I know aren't sorry for me."

"What are you talking about, Estelle?"

"Gracious Me and Balls Off aren't sorry for me."

"I'm not sorry for you, either."

"Anyone in his right mind would be," she said. "Goodbye."

"I'm sorry for you, but I'm just as sorry for —"

"Mokuaweoweo," she said.

"Me," he told the dial tone.

He took off his clothes, got under the sheet, and tried to sleep. He was too restless and down to sleep, so he sat up, pulled out the Manhattan phone directory from under his bed, and looked up the number of Lightning Strikes. He left a message with the bartender that Zappy Zoo Land did not know where Miss Dune could order any snakes.

He propped pillows behind his head and read an account by Raymond Ditmars of a twenty-foot python eating an eighty-pound pig. He read Ditmars's description of Australian marsupials, and the Elapine snakes in Africa. He read a bent Leonard Cohen poem about blood in the sink and humping the thorny crucifix and digging for grins in the tooth pile.

Then he read several chapters of *The Inheritors*. Stephen Gaunt, the whiz kid of Sinclair Broadcasting was making out with Green-eyed Girl, Blond Girl, Chinese Girl, Golden Girl, Darling Girl, Italian Girl, and Lawyer Girl.

In the midst of it, the phone rang.

"How are you, love?" Mother Girl said.

"I'll live."

"It doesn't sound worth the effort. What's the matter?"

"Nothing is."

"Something is. How was your party? Are you taking good care of Loretta?"

"Albert's taking good care of Loretta."

"Well, you asked for that, Sydney. Why did you invite Estelle down the same weekend you asked Loretta in?"

"It doesn't really matter," he said. "How are things in Quogue?"

"I'm not in Quogue, love. That's what I called to tell you. Liz and I drove up to Westport late last night. Annie isn't feeling well."

"What about Quogue?"

"I just told you. I'm not in Quogue. I'm not going to Quogue."

"Aren't they expecting you in Quogue?"

"They were, but I had to call them and tell them Annie's ill."

"Are you going to spend the whole weekend in Westport?"

"I'll drive back Sunday afternoon."

"And not go to Quogue at all?"

"I'll be here in Westport if you want me. Now *what's* with you? Is Loretta angry with you?"

"No."

"Estelle?"

"No."

"Then stop sulking around, Sydney. I can tell by your voice you're sulking."

"Was," he said.

As soon as he finished the conversation with his mother, he put on white bell-bottoms and white shoes and a gray T-shirt. He took his gray blazer from the closet, and stuffed twenty dollars into his wallet. Then he wrote Loretta Willensky a note explaining he was suddenly called away.

By eight-thirty he was on Montauk Highway, en route to Quogue and Bryn Mawr Girl.

"*Where?*" she said.

"Right here. Quogue," he said. "In a gas station."

"Oh, Sydney, really?"

"Really."

"Sydney, everything is super-awful."

"Nothing is super-awful, Alison."

"Yes, it is."

"What's so super-awful?"

"Annie was going to *kill* herself over Ellie, Sydney!"

"So that's why my mother went to Westport."

"Shep had to rush up there. There've been all these phone calls back and forth. This has really been gross."

"Annie *didn't* kill herself, did she?"

"She would have, Sydney."

"I said she *didn't*, did she?"

"She was super-close to doing it, Sydney."

"She didn't do it, Alison."

"She didn't do it, but Shep went up there, and now here I am with people I hardly know and —"

"Alison?"

"What?"

"Calm down."

"That's easy for you to say, Sydney."

"Just calm down."

"You don't know what we've all been through, what I've been through. Sydney?"

"What?"

"It's good to hear your voice, Sydney."

"It's good to hear yours."

"You don't know what I've been through, Sydney. This has been really gross. I've never been *through* anything like this, and I even forgot my pot. I left it behind in the refrigerator. Oh God. Sydney?"

"What?"

"Oh God. I just thought of something on top of everything else."

"*What?*"

"Did you leave a note for the maid to defrost?"

"No."

"*No?* That's not a modern refrigerator, Sydney. If that refrigerator isn't defrosted, it breaks, and now I'm going to have a repair bill to pay."

"You're right," he said.

"Then why couldn't you have remembered to leave a note? I had to pay her a dollar seventy-five to work on the Fourth, too."

"I don't mean about the refrigerator," he said. "I mean you're right about the straitjacket, about needing something to hold you together."

"Did I say that? Sydney, I was stoned when I said that."

"What about when you wrote it to Raoul? What about when you made it into a little poem for my mother?"

"What?"

"You heard me, Alison."

"Sydney Skate, you're super-snoopy. I mean that. You are gross. Does Shep know you saw that?"

"*Shep* hasn't seen that. Somebody else slept in Shep's bed last night, Alison. Shep stayed at Liz's and Loretta Willensky slept in her bed. And Loretta Willensky decided I wrote that poem to her."

"Did she keep the book, too?"

"Right. The book that Raoul gave you and you gave my mother is now Loretta Willensky's gift from me," he said.

Lear calls you Youth Explosion. You're chicken in their eyes, Alison. They're all laughing at my mother because she's turned down chicken lane."

"You're doing it again, Sydney. You're trying to expose me to myself."

"Don't you want to know the truth?"

"Alison?"

"What?"

"We could go home and defrost the refrigerator, smoke some Acapulco Gold, and play with Dr. Teregram. We could stop for steamers on the way."

"Oh Sydney."

"What are you doing there in the first place?"

"I was invited."

"You know what I mean."

"Sydney, I promised them I'd go to some place called Linger with them."

"Fay Foote's place."

"I can't hurt their feelings."

"What about my feelings?"

"I didn't promise I'd go to Linger with you, Sydney."

"When I heard you were stranded, I drove out here to get you."

"They're drinking, Sydney."

"They drink."

"Why do they drink so much? They've been drinking since noon."

"It's not your age group."

"Do you know what they call getting your period? Getting the curse. I think I'm going to get my period any second and that's what's making me so uptight. Sydney, I have to hang up."

"Did you hear me? I drove out here to get you."

"I don't see how you can do that gracefully, Sydney. That would be super-sneaky."

"I don't want to go back without you," he said.

"We can't hurt Shep, Sydney; how can we? Sydney, they're getting ready to leave. I have to hang up, Sydney. I'm super-confused, so don't add to it, please."

At eleven o'clock Shockproof sat at the bar in Linger, drinking a third Dewar's and water. The real action in Linger was just about to begin. The checkroom girl informed him of this as she sat beside him, putting X's on quarters with red nail polish. This was one of her duties, to mark the house quarters so the jukebox owners would return them to Linger, and to keep the music playing as the place began to fill up.

Linger was a strange name for the cavernous room with its black walls and ceiling and flashing psychedelic lights. The lights gave a phosphorescent glow to people's clothes; the room seemed like one of M.E.'s old detergent ads where shirts and blouses danced around by themselves. No one at a distance seemed to have arms, hands, necks or faces. The music was loud — hard rock. The bartenders were hustlers, picking up half-full drinks and dumping them down drains. The small dance floor was packed with gyrating couples. Cigarette smoke settled over the room

like a fog, and all the matchbooks bore the inscription
Linger, Swinger.

Shockproof was watching the door nervously, waiting
for Alison with that sinking feeling that she wouldn't
show up. He was wary, too, of when she would, of how
they would all behave toward him now that he had in-
vaded their territory for the first time. While he watched
people enter Linger, he remembered an old John Collier
story about department store mannequins entertaining at
dances after all the help and customers went home. So
many faces seemed waxen and of no definitive age. There
was a strange, stylized hyper-enthusiasm in the exchanges
between small groups of females and males, who seemed
always to enter separately, then discover each other with
extravagant joy: males lifting females off the floor in
wrestling embraces, many grand mouth-to-mouth kisses,
accompanied by shouts of "darling," "love," like this room
was some fun-filled Garden of Eden where males and females were encountering one another for the first time.
Shockproof knew it all for what it was: code.

Then a very familiar voice said, "Leave, or I'm going to
have you bounced, Sydney."

"Hello, Corita."

She was deeply tanned, wearing a white linen dress
which glowed splendorously and was embellished at the
bosom V by a large, round, gold, sign-of-Capricorn medal-
lion. She had short, shaggy brown hair with piercing
brown eyes and an expression of anger he remembered

well from times he would not straighten up his room, eat salad of any kind, or put down what he was reading immediately, to answer her summons to the dinner table.

"Did you hear what I said, Sydney? You're underage."

"I'll switch to Coke. I'm waiting for someone."

"She's not coming, Sydney. She doesn't feel well."

"Where is she?"

"You know where she is. She's at Ellie's and Gloria's. She wants to be by herself."

"Where's their place?"

"She wants to be by herself, Sydney. Why don't you go back to New York now?"

"No," he said.

"Shep doesn't know you're out here, does she?"

"No."

"Why don't you go back to New York now, and leave it that way?"

"Where's their place?"

"Sydney, don't make me call the bouncer. Let's not have a scene here."

"Then tell me how to get to Alison."

"If she'd wanted you to get to her, she would have given you instructions when you talked to her."

"She's confused."

"I agree. But it doesn't have anything to do with you."

"I know what's going on," he said.

"When didn't you, Sydney?" she said. "You've got five minutes to pay up and leave. Stick to the rules, Sydney.

Don't make everyone including yourself uncomfortable."

Actually it took ten minutes for the bouncer to show up and escort him from Linger. Shockproof put up a struggle and was dragged toward the door shouting out denunciations, while he caught chaotic glimpses of familiar faces: Judy Ewen, Gloria Roy, Ellie Davies, Victor and Paul — then he was picking himself up from the gravel driveway, brushing off the knees of his bell-bottoms.

Victor was walking rapidly toward him. "Hey, Sydney. Are you all right? For God's sake. I *couldn't* be angrier with Corita. She didn't have to do it *that* way."

He brushed off the sleeve of Shockproof's blazer. "Are you all *right*?"

"Yes."

"Whew! Sydney! You really let fly. I hope you didn't *mean* all that."

"All what?" Shockproof said shrugging, alternately trying to go back on code, and to remember who he was in what novel . . . and he became Dustin Hoffman playing *The Graduate*, out to capture Elaine Robinson by sheer persistence, by relentless, stubborn, clumsy endurance. "Where's Alison, Victor?"

"She didn't come in with them, Sydney. She's probably at Ellie's and Gloria's."

"Where's their place?"

"Next to Judy Ewen's on Dune Road. . . . Sydney. For God's sake, *don't* tell Shep *I* got involved in this. I don't want to be in the middle. Lord. What a situ-*ation*."

But he was smiling very faintly, and Shockproof smiled back at him.

"Thanks, Victor."

Shockproof knew the way, and drove carefully through the fog envisioning Benjamin, the Graduate, slamming his hand down on the railing of the church balcony, yelling, "Elaine!!!"

The organ music stopped.

He slammed his hands down again. "Elaine!!! Elaine!!! Elaine!!!"

The fog grew thicker and he drove down the winding side roads very carefully, unable to believe that despite the emotional debris he had brought about and then left behind him, despite the unimaginable consequences of the scene in Linger, and the palpitations of his heart, there was a pleasurable physical stirring near his groin at the thought of finally reaching Alison.

He remembered her saying over the phone that she thought she was going to get her period any second, and Corita telling him she didn't feel well. He definitely wanted her, and he began to count on the fact that it wouldn't make any difference if she had her period, as it never had when Estelle had hers, but he became hung up momentarily on a part of *Good Time Coming* by Edmund Schiddel. He remembered when Anson Parris hurried down to Neile Eythe's Mott Street apartment that afternoon, on impulse, and told Neile how he wanted her.

"Can't have today," she said.

"Why not?"

"Because — you know."

"I hate 'you know.' Why should there be 'you know' between us?"

"I can't because — my glimpse of the moon, you fool!"

"I'm sorry," he said again, comprehending.

No.

No one under thirty would try and pull that, and coming in from the fog he coupled with her, passing the firehouse now, watching the curves, passing Judy Ewen's, where those at Linger had left their cars: he could see them lined up in the driveway. He cut his motor, switched off his lights, and got out of the T-bird. The house was lit, the front porch light on, and he walked through the wet grass to the door, letting himself in quietly. He was about to call out to her when he heard her giggle.

". . . and I told her that, too" — Fay Foote's voice — "everything I'm telling you now."

"God. You're gross. What'd she *say*?"

Fay Foote imitated M.E. "Fay. Listen. *You're* jaded. Really."

"God. You're a super-marvelous mimic. I can just *hear* her."

"I said, Shep: (*a*) these so-called bisexual little girls who hang around my places are the shit at the rodeo, and (*b*) you don't have to protect these young kids today, you have to protect yourselves from them."

A squeal.

"I said, Shep: these kids are *years* ahead of us, and anyway you always had a morality that dated back to the Punic Wars."

"I did a paper on Punica *fides*, contrasting it with Attic faith. Just last year."

"Shep said that's better than no morality at all."

"I hate morality. It's super-beside-the-point."

"We're on the same wavelength, baby."

"God. All this time I've been showing Shep the emotion I feel for you. I can see that now."

"I turn you on, don't I?"

"Mucho mucho."

"Then come on over here."

"First tell me I'm not the shit at the rodeo."

"I'll just tell you that we're not at a rodeo right now. How's that?"

Someone got up and walked across the living room floor, pausing just long enough to turn up the hi-fi.

For a few seconds longer Shockproof stood in the entranceway, staring into the dining room where the coffee cups and dinner plates and wineglasses had been left uncleared. He started to leave, unnoticed, as he had arrived, but before he left he took a few steps forward and yanked the tablecloth and everything atop it to the floor.

He didn't look back toward the living room, or say anything, or hear anything after that. He got into his car and headed home.

13   *we did not go out /
we did not feel happy*

What got him through the weekend was Jordan
Legier's paintbox theory in *Good Times, Bad Times,*
which he read Saturday morning, after Loretta Willensky
went off to Jones Beach with Albert.

The Big Joker in the sky presents all people with a
paintbox for use during their stay on earth; everyone uses
his paintbox to make the pictures of his life: learning,
working, love, marriage, etc. Except no one's paintbox is

the same. Some are beautiful and fully equipped, but in some a brush is twisted or missing altogether. In others, even primary colors are not included. A few paintboxes will not even open. . . . Yet everyone must depend on the paintbox he received from the Big Joker: that is his sole equipment for his life.

Shockproof wrote Joel Schwartz a letter detailing the paintbox theory, though he was not in the habit of corresponding with him. He started to write his father the same sort of letter, but changed his mind and instead sent off something about his appreciation of how his father and Rosemary must have suffered because of her inability to have children (". . . see now the pathetic reasoning behind your choice of the name 'Daughter' for the cat"). He was eager to write Estelle Kelly, but he had no idea where in Hawaii she was, and imagined anyway that the Captain would intercept and destroy any letter from him to her.

He imagined that somehow he would work in the paintbox theory during the confrontation with M.E. at the end of the weekend, though he was not sure how he would use it: in her defense, or in his own, or as a summation to whatever it was they would say to one another. The confrontation loomed as unpredictable and unfathomable in his mind as the future itself. He found himself measuring time so that forty-eight hours from a certain minute that future would be past, three months from this day that past well past, and in a year barely remembered.

Early Saturday morning, Cappy had called, chatted ten minutes with him in her usual way, but he felt after the phone call that she was acting for M.E., who by then had surely received telephone reports from Quogue, and probably asked Cappy to check on him.

The paintbox theory carried him along. It was in his thoughts as he flushed a deceased salamander down the toilet at Zappy Zoo Land, and as he walked to and from work across Fourteenth Street with its sad and grotesque carnival of the unbeautiful people, and as he read *Steps* by Jerzy Kosinski, unable to make sense of it or become uninvolved in it, convinced the italicized dialogue scattered through it was the way people with the best paintboxes talked to each other — no wonder it seemed beautiful and mysterious and desirable.

"*. . . Simply give yourself up to what you feel: enjoy that awareness. Lovers are not snails; they don't have to protrude from their shells and meet each other halfway. Meet me within your own self.*"

"*I never thought of it as you see it; that would not come naturally to me. But you, what do you feel?*"

"*I want you, you alone. But beyond you and me together, I see myself in our love-making. It is this vision of myself as your lover I wish to retain and make more real.*"

He could not read too much of *Steps* at one time, would put it down and pick up *Listen to the Silence*, living in the clang of locking asylum doors with fourteen-year-old Timmy, running through that loony bin carrying trays to the girls' building, with the sausages cut up so the girls wouldn't use them at night.

On Sunday afternoon Loretta Willensky thanked him politely for the weekend, and Albert drove her back to Bucks County in Mike's car. Shockproof read many books at the same time, paced, and watched for M.E.'s Mercedes.

He had made up a sentence about Alison. Finally you have hurt me more than I love you. But he did not believe in either thing, the hurt or the love, though he liked the sentence and wrote it down on a slip of paper, imagining as he did that anything like that he had ever read had been written by someone insensitive enough to remember pain or joy so well that he could describe it.

The entire weekend had one focus: M.E.'s arrival, and most of the conversations in his head were between M.E. and himself, endless variations with vastly different approaches, and moods swinging from solemn to blithe, rejecting to uncensuring. He planned and planned it, yet when she finally let herself in the front door shortly after eleven Sunday evening, he was irritated that she had interrupted *Island Princess* with Marcello Mastroianni, which he was watching on television.

"Are you decent?"

"Yes. Come on in."

She was wearing a light blue Lilly and sunglasses, which she took off, and then slipped out of her Swedish clogs as she sat down in the leather chair near his desk. "Are you watching something?"

"No. It's dubbed, anyway." He turned down the sound on the set.

She lit a Gauloise. "The traffic was murder."

"Albert drove Loretta back."

"Is this a new romance?"

"I suppose."

"Shall I check with the service, or did you get the calls?"

"There weren't any. Cappy called."

"Sydney, I think I'm going to take my vacation early. I'll probably leave Wednesday."

"Where are you going?"

"Liz and Annie and I are going to St. Thomas for two weeks."

"Good enough."

"If I can get the Gun people off my back, I'll leave Wednesday night."

"Okay."

"That must have been made years ago."

"1955, according to *Cue*. Before anyone even knew Mastroianni."

"When I get back we'll have to shop for college. You need a new winter coat. Winters are hell upstate."

"I could get one of those things where the lining zips out and use it for spring and winter."

"We'll do all that when I get back."

"Cappy's going to the Cape tomorrow."

"I know. I want to call her before it's too late. I'll do that now." She picked up her clogs and stood up. "Sydney?"

"What?"

"Are things okay between us?"

"Yes."

"Is there anything you want to discuss?"

"Nothing."

"I want to check over your luggage, too. I think you could use a new footlocker."

"I need boots."

"I know. We'll do all that when I get back. I'm going to fix a sandwich. Do you want one?"

"I ate already."

On and on.

Passing for any other conversation, save for those few seconds, so fleeting and unexpected that he could not be sure he had not imagined it, or read it in some novel and then interjected it into the proceedings. How had it gone exactly? *Are things okay?/Yes./Is there anything to say?/Nothing.*

Monsieur Meursault heard the judge's voice asking him if he had anything more to say. After thinking for a moment, Meursault answered "No." Then the policemen led him out.

Later he heard her across the hall, telling Cappy over the telephone: "No, on the contrary. I think I'm relieved." But he did not know what it was she was relieved over: the Alison thing, or this thing. He turned off *Island Princess*, and there was silence in the house for some time while Cappy talked and M.E. listened, occasionally said, "Yes," "I know," "Ummm hmmm." She knew that he could hear, and he thought of closing his bedroom door, but she had not closed hers; he left it open, picked up *Steps* again,

half read, half heard M.E.'s incidental remarks as Cappy
did the talking.

Then M.E. began to talk: about Annie's suicide threat,
and how she and Liz had gone directly to Westport after
their phone conversation with Annie, about their plans for
the trip to St. Thomas, on and on, until Shockproof began
to feel comfortable with the hum of gossip emanating
from M.E.'s room, and something to read: now, in *Steps*,
the hero had found a disguise, that of a deaf-mute, and he
acted out his wishes in pantomime, and this notion dis-
tracted Shockproof somewhat, so that it was some time
before it registered with him that M.E. was not bothering
to use code: ". . . the pity of it is," she was telling Cappy,
"there's just no way now to convince Annie that she'll ever
love another woman as she loves Ellie."

Before she left for St. Thomas, M.E. never went back on
code, and often as Shockproof adjusted to this new way of
life, he remembered the hero in *Steps* jerking his shoulders and flapping his ear like a spastic, to indicate to
people that he could not hear and could not speak. Once,
when M.E. remarked at breakfast that one reason for the
St. Thomas trip was so Ellie could move her things out of
the house in Annie's absence (". . . sparing Annie that
heartbreak"), he found his hand feeling his ear, remembering how in the deaf-mute charade, the ear was slapped
repeatedly until people perceived the defect.

He said, "It's such a beautiful house. Won't Ellie miss
it?"

"Yes. Sure."

A week from the day she left, he spent the day unpacking a shipment of rabbits. One large fawn-colored Flemish Giant was nibbling on the hay in her box, forming it into a nest and pulling out the hair from her own body, to conscientiously line the nest. It was a sign she was pregnant, and he separated her from the others, leaving a note about her condition for Leogrande, since the next day was his day off. He checked in the order book on Leogrande's desk to be sure ZZL was still filling the standard order for mice and ribbon snakes at Gray, A., on Gramercy Park South. As always, he made sure there was no mail from Lorna Dune.

On his way home, he stopped at the stationer's and selected a Morton Cooper, *The French Lieutenant's Woman*, and a Catherine Gaskin gothic from the lending library.

An invoice from his father awaited him at home.

Dear Sydney,
Yours of 7 July received. "Daughter" was named before we bought her from Morton Goldman. Your stepmother is now visiting her sister in Jacksonville, Florida. With all its beaches and natural facilities, more swimming pools are sold in that state per annum than in Pennsylvania and New Jersey put together. Will we see you before you leave for college?
Affectionately,
Your father, Harold Skate.

He was living largely in the back of the house, save for brief intervals in the kitchen and bathroom. He made himself a peanut butter sandwich and opened a bottle of Dr. Brown's Cel-Ray, then carried it into M.E.'s bedroom and sat on the chaise staring at her personal bookshelf. The den contained most of their books, but they both had a private collection in their bedrooms; they had an understanding that they would not borrow from each other's private collection.

In M.E.'s absence he often looked through her personal books, knowing her habit of filing letters and mementos in particular volumes. For example, several notes and a few theater stubs dating back from the period with Cappy were contained in a slender red book of Charlotte Mew's *Collected Poems;* there were two letters from Corita Carr in *Crime and Punishment.* There was a valentine from someone named Clarissa in Curzio Malaparte's *Kaputt.* At school, he had imitated M.E.'s system and filed letters from Estelle Kelly in *'Tis Pity She's a Whore,* and a few of his father's invoices in Voltaire's *Philosophical Dictionary.*

He munched on his sandwich and opened a dozen books, finding nothing new. He weighed the idea of going through every book, then changed his mind and went back across the hall to his own room.

For a while he watched Mike, Albert and Hippy Hair attempt Greek dances down in the garden; then he shut the window and turned on the air conditioning. He had seen too many of those new movies where the characters' pasts kept flashing jerkily across the screen out of context, and he fought the impulse to pretend he was in a film and that was happening to him. He fought any confirmation coming from his end that he was down, and was in fact laughing sometime later when the phone rang. He had just found the part in *The French Lieutenant's Woman* when prim, pale, Ernestina wrote in her black morocco diary (with the gold clasp): *Did not see dearest Charles. Did not go out. Did not feel happy.*

"Did not expect to hear from you," he told Estelle.

"The coast is clear," she said. "The password is 'Found Under Carnal Knowledge' — that's the derivation of fuck, in case nobody hopped off a tram and told you. They used it in British Army medical reports — cor, fancy *that*. I learned a terrible lot in Merry Old Hawaii."

"Where are Gracious Me and Balls Off?" he said.

"Points west by jet. Do you know what Cock Robin's name was before he changed it?"

"Why don't you come down here? My mother's away."

"Penis Rabinowitz. . . . How soon?"

"Anytime. I don't have to work tomorrow."

"Splashdown in forty-five minutes," she said. "Advise the Lunar Receiving Laboratory to stand by for rock samples, and ready the mobile quarantine facility."

Near midnight she was Black Star under Warren Webber, squeezing the hard, hot velvet instrument: *He was stroking her slowly, with certainty, with man's certainty, and she bit his chin with her teeth and wanted the velvet to burst inside her, wanted it to velvet her forever, wanted it, wanted it O God I've never had it like this, wanted it, I'll die if it doesn't happen now. I'll die if you stop, want it, want it, deeper, fuller, slower, need it, faster now —*

"Stop pumping, you're not even in me!" said Estelle.

"I'll build us another drink," said Warren Webber.

But on the way to the kitchen, like a sudden attack of hiccups, he heard himself sob, the sensation arresting him momentarily in the narrow hallway. The sound came like stabs. He leaned against the wall. They were hoarse, staccato, unpremeditated sounds, which he quickly transformed into the noise of a coughing fit.

Then he got past it.

"Do you want to know why I didn't radio in for takeoff clearance this morning, Navigator?" They were walking toward Third Avenue to hail a taxi for Estelle. It was a sunny, summer noon; he planned to go back home after he caught a cab for her, and sleep off his hangover.

"Why didn't you?"

"Because I didn't wake up with an octopus." Estelle was jumping the cracks in the sidewalk on Nineteenth Street, swinging a green straw bag with *MAUNA LOA, Hawaii National Park* threaded through its side in yellow.

He started to say something when he saw Alison Gray. She was in her Triumph, with the top down, waiting for the light on the corner of Nineteenth and Third. Beside her, in the front seat, was a chunky fellow with long black curly sideburns, and those goggle-like large round yellow spectacles.

"For once you didn't have hangover hots," Estelle said. "You actually stayed on your own side of the bed. Did you heave in the night or something?"

Then Alison looked toward him.

"Are we on the same wavelength this morning?" Estelle asked. "Pilot to tower, pilot to tower, can you read me?"

"I see someone," he said.

Alison waved at him, and in an instant he was saying: *"They make good pets."*

"This one smells. He's really super-stinky."

"He's making himself smell."

"Huh?"

"He's doing it on purpose."

"How gross."

"He does it on purpose." Shockproof became hotly aware of the fact she had very large breasts for such a tall, thin girl.

The light changed, the Triumph headed down Third.

"What's the *matter* with you?" Estelle complained.

"I was being Richard Chamberlain in *Petulia,* having a sudden vision of my wretched, meaningful past. Click click. The present. Click click. The past."

"Piss off," she said. "Do you know who Gracious Me *idolizes*? Glen Campbell. Because he asks his mother and father to be on his show. She likes Jug Ears, too."

"Who?"

"Julie and Jug Ears. Click click. The future. Hail to the Chief: Jug Ears and the Swatch Off the Old Cloth Coat."

"Click. Click. The future," Shockproof said. "The South Vietnamese government announced today that its armed forces have increased eight hundred men during the past seven years, a factor presumably in the six-hundredth withdrawal of American troops President Eisenhower will announce later this month."

They click-clicked and laughed through two empty cabs; then they stopped one, she got in, and Shockproof walked back home uncertainly trying to keep his thoughts just left or right of focus.

Waiting for him on the front steps was the chunky fellow he had seen just a short time ago in the Triumph with Alison.

"I'm Raoul Miller." He reached for Shockproof's hand.

14 *knifing suddenly slickly*

"I don't suppose you've heard about Alison?" Raoul began.

Some idiotic conversation had preceded this one, as Shockproof was leading him into the den; it had been about parking in New York, meter maids, and tow-away fees. Raoul, out front, had asked: "Is there someplace we can talk?"

"What about Alison?" Shockproof said. He supposed this was the showdown he had been headed for ever since

Quogue. No more vague passes at it, as though Fate were some punch-drunk boxer always missing the bag. Now the knuckle on the leather at last. Otherwise, what had Raoul come here for?

Raoul had a white G-shaped pipe which he was packing. He was letting the question hang, while he scratched a match to light the pipe. Shockproof could not imagine him naked making love, or sending off a telegram signed *Found* (which implied at one point he'd been lost); he could not imagine him in a foursy, or deserving that first name. Norman was more like it; Howard; Kenneth.

"I don't know how much you really know about Ali," said Raoul, sucking the pipe.

"Not a great deal." Let him be the one to blurt it all out; Shockproof was not going to admit anything. But he resented his calling her "Ali," as though he knew some third face of Eve Shockproof didn't know. Oh, Shockproof knew her; he knew her all right.

"Ali and her urgencies and her crises," Raoul said, "and yes, her élan."

Shockproof had his own urgencies: hangover thirst was one. To brush his teeth. To sleep.

"Ali," said Raoul, "and her compulsive adventurousness."

Leading up to the truth, ah?

Your mother did —

Your mother is —

You are —

Click click.

Edens Lost; Angus asking Eve: *"Aren't you ever affected, ever touched by anything?"*

"I would have to think about that."

"In all the years I've known you, I've only seen you thrown once."

"Yes, well, that was unforgivable."

"Do you mean," Angus asked leisurely, *"killing the dog was? Or do you mean your giving away to hysterical behavior was unforgivable?"*

"A few days ago her father called me," Raoul said.

"Yes, and?" Shockproof said leisurely.

"From the coast."

"And?"

"I can't say I was surprised." Shockproof felt like telling Raoul he didn't care whether or not Raoul could say he was surprised; keep out of it, Raoul, Shockproof felt like saying.

"He said he'd received a call from Ali. She'd started off the conversation by saying she was lucky she had ten fingers, because it had taken nine to dial the number. Each time she dialed a digit, she imagined she'd lost a finger. She said she only had one left. Have you ever dropped mescaline, Sydney?"

"No," Shockproof said, and then — just as Raoul had said a moment before — Shockproof said, "I can't say I'm surprised."

"I'd hoped Ali was finished with those sophomorics."

"But she's all right. I saw her in the car."

"All right," said Raoul, exactly as Alison used to repeat

words Shockproof would say, to show how far off target he was: "You look nice" — "*Nice*," she would say; "What's the matter?" — "*What's the matter*," she would say.

Raoul said, "Well. She survived her trip, if that's what you mean. It was a bummer. She was by herself. I got in touch with a doctor here in New York. He helped her, gave her Thorazine, hospitalized her. I flew in from Boston; her family flew in from L.A."

"I just saw her," Shockproof blurted out again.

"Yes. I know. That's why I'm here. She's at the apartment with her folks." He glanced at his watch. "Probably by now getting ready to leave for Kennedy with her father. She's going back to L.A. with him."

Mercifully, the telephone rang. Shockproof ran to the back of the house to answer it, knowing that after the call he could slip into the kitchen and down some ice water. The call was from the garage on Irving Place; M.E.'s Mercedes had undergone its checkup and was ready to be transferred to her regular garage on Twentieth Street. In the kitchen Shockproof quenched his thirst. When the knuckle connected with the leather, would he react? Defend M.E.? Share blame? Why? — when Alison had done this whole damn thing to both of them. Her "urgencies"; her "compulsive adventurousness" — shit.

He went back to the den. Raoul was on his feet inspecting the bookshelves, the way certain people enter a room, and in a studied, obvious way, pretend to be sizing up the person whose room it is, by taking in every picture, plant and wall plug.

"She hopes you're not angry with her," said Raoul, continuing his survey of the books. "And I think she means it, though it's hard to tell when someone's so polymorphous-perverse, what's sincere and what isn't."

"Poly what?"

"Polymorphous-perverse," said Raoul. "Perverse in all directions, as a child is. One of Freud's theories." He turned around and stuck one hand into the pocket of his trousers, jangling his change. "I know everything that's been going on, everything. Sydney, Ali's very disturbed."

He said it with the same emphasis Loretta Willensky had used in describing Estelle Kelly. Dis-*turbed*.

"I suppose so," Shockproof said feebly.

"It's easy to be taken in by her," said Raoul. "It's the strange paradox about borderline psychotics. It's easier to be taken in by them than it is by neurotics. They have a better façade because they aren't any longer building defenses. Instead, they're going along with their fantasies; the fantasy life takes over, and they seem more relaxed and unconfused. Actually, they are more relaxed and unconfused. They've turned off."

Shockproof sat down in M.E.'s leather chair. He couldn't think of anything to say.

"Has she ever told you that she didn't want to hurt you, or that she had to do something because she didn't want to hurt someone?"

"I suppose so," Shockproof said. "Yes."

"It was Ali she didn't want to hurt, but she was too far removed from her superego to perceive that."

Silence.

Shockproof said, "What's she going to do?"

"She'll get some professional help."

"I thought she was already getting that."

"She doesn't really qualify anymore as a general analysand."

Whatever *that* meant.

What? The loony bin? Timmy in *Listen to the Silence* living with the clang of locking doors, wire cages, peeling paint; the sausages cut up so the women wouldn't —

Right now: *stop.*

"Do you know this Fay Foote?" Raoul said.

"Not well."

"What? I didn't hear you."

"She's some dyke." He had never used the word before.

"She has Ali's makeup kit. It's not an expensive thing, not anything that couldn't be replaced, but Ali wants it back. That's one of her symptoms: her obsession with material things, money."

"I could call her up, I guess, if she wants it so much."

"I'll give you Ali's address in L.A. She can send it there."

Then he began to talk about his affection, his more-than-affection for Ali; the fact he was once going to marry her; how he had dismissed so many warning signals; you don't see them in someone close to you, do you? On and on.

Shockproof remembered a woman M.E. was seeing for a time, in between Cappy and Corita. She was very beautiful, named Lauraine. She was always calling on the telephone at odd hours in the early morning, sending so many different bouquets at one time that the florist had to use two boys to deliver all of them; special deliveries, telegrams, on and on.

Her code name was "Lawrence." There was always gossip about Lawrence. Lawrence cracked up his XKE in Provincetown; Lawrence turned over an entire table full of food one night at Joe Allen's; Lawrence sang along with Carol Channing during a performance of *Hello, Dolly!* until the ushers removed him bodily from the theater. Oh God, that *Lawrence.* At times M.E. would double over laughing, tears rolling down her cheeks.

Suddenly, so it seemed, M.E. had instructed Shockproof to tell Lauraine she was not at home when Lauraine telephoned; then M.E. had their telephone number changed and listed privately. One day in M.E.'s address book, Lauraine's name, address and phone number were inked out with a Markette. The last gossip he had heard of Lawrence was that he was at Cool Breeze, in Connecticut. "Actually at Cool Breeze," as Corita Carr had put it. "Come *on!* We saw it coming."

"Well, Sydney," Raoul said. "I guess you know what I've come here about?"

"Come here about?" Shockproof was still caught up in the memory of Lauraine; now shaken from it and unable to comprehend what could possibly follow.

Raoul said, "You'll see to the snake, hmmm? It's driving Mrs. Gray up the wall, and she has to pack Ali's things."

She was not at all what he expected Alison's mother to be like. She was short and bosomy with very thin legs, and a choppy, almost militant gait. She was carrying various articles of clothing from the bedroom to the living room. She had long fingers and seemed unwilling to use more than the first one on her right hand and her thumb to deposit Alison's things into a large steamer trunk near the door. She had the attitude of some missionary dutifully cleaning out a leper's lair. Her expression was sour and tumid, and she gave Shockproof as much attention as she might have accorded a tradesman's assistant, unable even to manage a nod when Shockproof entered with Raoul. Raoul did not introduce them either.

The television was playing on the table: *Hannibal,* starring Victor Mature and Rita Gam.

"I can't take both the snake and the cage now," Shockproof told Raoul. "I'll have to take the snake now, and then come back for the cage."

"You're going to take the snake in your hands?" she said.

"You're a better man than I am, Gunga Din," Raoul chuckled, as Shockproof opened the top of the cage.

"Hello, Dr. Teregram."

"Don't *call* it that," said Mrs. Gray. "Forty dollars an hour, three times a week; it's not my idea of a joke." Again, she was talking to no one in particular.

"He probably has to," Raoul said. "The thing probably knows its name."

"They don't have ears," said Shockproof. "It's just a habit."

"Alison said she fed it yesterday," Raoul said.

"*Fed* it," Mrs. Gray said in a disgusted tone to the steamer trunk.

"She wanted you to know that," Raoul said.

Shockproof picked up the King, looped her across his shoulder.

"Oh, and wait!" Raoul said, disappearing a moment.

Shockproof waited. Across the television screen came Ann MacReynolds, playing the female computer, waltzing off with the black-masked, silver-sabered box of Porproganni spaghetti.

Raoul reappeared. "Ali wanted you to have this."

It was the board with the mottled snake skin attached, which she had mounted herself and shellacked.

Shockproof parked the Mercedes on Central Park West, and walked east toward Belvedere Castle and the Revolutionary War forts and the sloping, ledgy hills and cliffs. People turned and looked back at him as he passed carrying the King. The decision to bring her here had not been made carefully, though he supposed some intuitive thought process had evolved from all that had happened since summer began. It would never have occurred to him to let her go at the beginning of the summer. He would have caged her, cared for her meticulously, sparing her fungus, mites, dampness. He would have tortured himself

with insomnial visions of Lorna Dune getting hold of h

He was still uncertain that it was the right decisio
and not sure he could go through with it. He thought o
pointing himself in the direction of the zoo instead, oi
handing her over to someone there for safekeeping.

Cancer Ward.

Remember when Oleg was released from the hospital,
his visit to the zoo? The sign on the white owl's cage: *"The
white owl endures captivity with difficulty."*

They know it — and still they imprison him.

The black bear poking his nose at the wire of the cage,
then suddenly jumping up and just clinging there desper-
ately; the polar bear in the hundred-degree heat; the deer
without running space; the sacred Indian zebu cow behind bars; the agouti, the monkeys; the eyes of the nilgai
antelope, light brown, large, dear — like the eyes of Oleg's
lover, Vega — was it witchcraft, a transmigration of soul?
Vega asking, *"Can it be that you won't come?"*

He kneeled in the grass holding on to Dr. Teregram. He
thought of Alison aboard a plane, flying back to California
with her father, whom Shockproof had never seen and
could not even visualize.

Shockproof had the idea that it had all happened in a
dream, like life had happened in *Bruno's Dream* to Bruno
for nearly ninety years.

*It's all a dream . . . one goes through life in a dream,
it's all too hard. . . . There is no "it" for it to be all about.
There is just the dream, its texture, its essence, and in our*

last things we subsist only in the dream of another, a shade within a shade, fading, fading, fading.

Overhead a plane growing smaller and smaller in the blue sky, and old Bruno trying to save a fly from a spider with the strength left from dying. . . . Shockproof shook off the daydreams of books to try and deal with things. . . . Would she be all right? Would who be all right — Dr. Teregram or Alison? Would who be all right? And now he was back into Bruno's dying, unable to remember things, wondering if death was waking up from the dream.

Remember the letter to Joyce Carol Oates from the novel's heroine in the middle of *Them?* Maureen Wendall's letter complaining about books: *None of them ever happened. In my life something happened and I have to keep thinking about it over and over.*

He could take the King back to Nineteenth Street; he could convince M.E. to let him keep it until he found someone to care for it, or placed it with a reputable dealer.

There were cliffs nearby with crevices, secluded and tangled, with wild roots crisscrossed over them. Springs in Virginia on walks with Joel, he had seen whole bevies of heads of rattlers, copperheads and black snakes peering from slits in sun-warmed rocks.

Shockproof put the snake down on the grass.

Like all snakes, Dr. Teregram was not eager to move before she'd sized up the situation. Her head was up; she could have been a twisted stick lying in a field, except for the forked tongue darting in and out, investigating.

He imagined himself to be her, stood dead still, his tongue flickering lightly to smell the air, abruptly knifing suddenly slickly through the grass, pointing for the Egyptian obelisk near Eighty-fourth, gliding, gliding . . .

15   *home*

The next time Sydney Skate heard from Alison
Gray, it was Christmas. He was home for vacation. There
was a card from her with a lion cub on the front; on the
back in small print: *Proceeds from the sale of these cards
benefit the East African Wild Life Society.*

Inside Alison had written:

Dear Sydney,
*Seasons Greetings, as they say. I thought this card was just
right for you and looked for one with a snake on it, but I*

guess that would be too bent for Joyeux Noel. Sydney, I called Fay F. in October about my makeup kit and she said you had it. Do you? I really miss it. It's a Gucci and cost a lot. Tell everyone hello. Beaucoup love, Alison.

It was postmarked Armonk, New York.

Christmas Eve afternoon M.E. threw a big party, which she and Liz Lear prepared for two days ahead of time, cooking and decorating the house; forty guests were invited. Estelle Kelly had been asked, but Gracious Me would not allow her to attend, because Balls Off still disapproved of Sydney.

"He calls you 'the junkie,'" Estelle had written him while he was at Cornell, "so if you're going to write me, send the letter c/o Agatha Henry at Barnard, but if you're too busy getting head I'll sneak out Xmess Eve for a fast one with you in the local pub. The big news is Gracious Me is knocked up; one in the oven at her age!"

For a while, Sydney bartended the party. Ellie and Gloria were there; Judy Ewen and Corita; Fay Foote and her husband; Victor and Paul; Ann MacReynolds who was going with Cappy now; Roger Wolfe with his mother who was visiting from Memphis; on and on.

At one point, Mr. Boris climbed up on a hassock and asked everyone to be quiet; then he announced "the engagement of my daughter, Loretta, to Albert Allen Service. They'll be married at St. Thomas on Twelfth Night, next month."

There was applause and cheers, and Hippy Hair, who

was there with Mike and Deborah, serenaded the be-
trothed by playing "With a Little Help from My Friends"
on a comb covered with Zig Zag roll-your-own cigarette
paper.

Sydney was called away in the midst of this performance to take a telephone call in M.E.'s bedroom.

"Merry Christmas, son," said Harold Skate.

"Merry Christmas."

"Your stepmother and I are real proud of you. Morty
Goldman's over here, and I've been telling him about that
paper — Morty, this is Sydney on the phone. Pick up in
the kitchen, Morty. This is Sydney. I couldn't pronounce
that word, Sydney, but I was telling Morty about it. That's
his department. I told him you were a lab assistant in the
Zoology — Morty?"

"Merry Christmas, Sydney," a man's voice said. "Happy
Chanukah."

"Merry Christmas," Sydney said.

"Morty," Harold Skate said, "I want to introduce my
son, Sydney. Sydney, this is Dr. Goldman, our local zoolo-
gist."

"I'm only a vet," Goldman laughed. "How do you do,
Sydney."

"How do you do."

"What was that paper, Sydney? They're going to pub-
lish it, Morty, in some big scientific journal. Kid's only a
freshman in college."

"What's it about, Sydney?" Goldman said.

"Tell him, Sydney," said Harold Skate. "He's a lab as-

sistant, Morty. They usually give that job to grad students."

"What's it about, Sydney?" Goldman said.

"Parthenogenesis," said Sydney.

"Congratulations," said Goldman.

"Your stepmother's here. She wants to talk to you," said
Harold Skate.

"It's nice to meet you," said Goldman.

"Same here," Sydney said.

"Sydney?" said Rosemary Skate. "Did you get a notice of
your subscription?"

"Not yet, Rosemary."

"*National Geographic*, Sydney. Merry Christmas. We
got your package, but we don't open our presents until tomorrow morning, so we can't really thank you."

"Thank you," Sydney said. "Merry Christmas."

Harold Skate was back on the phone. "Sydney? Listen,
Sydney. You stick to your bugs and snakes and other animals. We don't need any geniuses in the swimming pool
business. I tell my customers I've got a son who's going to
be off in Norway someday collecting a Nobel Prize."

"Sweden, Hal! Sweden!" Goldman shouted in the background. "Stockholm."

"Anyway," said Harold Skate, "Merry Christmas, son."

"Thanks, Dad. Same to you and Rosemary."

When he hung up, Liz Lear was standing in the doorway. "You're fired, Sydney," she said.

"What?"

"Canned. This party no longer needs a bartender."

"I was going to quit anyway, for a while."

"Shep says you've got a date. You want to take my car?"

"I've got mine out front."

"Mine's got new snow tires."

"Thanks, anyway, but I haven't had any trouble," he said. "Hey, thanks for all the record albums, too, Liz."

"I get them for nothing, Sydney. It's graft."

Then M.E. appeared. "Liz, Gloria's getting very thick-tongued. Can you get some coffee into her?"

"I'll try, love. Where's Ellie, though?"

"She's moving her car to the garage on Irving Place. She can't do anything with her, anyway; *you're* the authority on Gloria Inhercups. . . . Sydney? It's snowing out. If you're going way up to Estelle's, why don't you take Liz's car? She's got new snow tires." M.E. added, "It's a Porsche, too, Sydney."

"Oh, I'll get there," Sydney said.

"You won't be late, will you?"

"I'll be back before this thing breaks up."

"Sydney, we'll open our gifts tomorrow," M.E. said. "Okay?"

"Okay."

"We'll clean up this mess later. Come back and help. Promise?"

"Promise."

"*Don't* forget. . . . Give your old ma a kiss"

Before he left, he reached into the huge crystal brandy snifter on M.E.'s bureau for matchbooks: O'Neal's, Maxwell's Plum, Daly's and West Boondock. For Christmas he had bought Estelle a gold frog pin with green eyes, which he had ordered from the Neiman-Marcus Christmas Book.

"Male frogs are real horny when they make out," he told Estelle, while they were sitting at the bar of the Boeuf à la Mode, near East End Avenue in the Eighties. "A male russet frog will leap on a female's back and squeeze like hell. You can do anything to him, touch him, tease him, even decapitate him — he won't let go. If the water's cold, he can hang on for weeks. Sometimes he squeezes so hard, he caves in the female's chest."

He was trying hard to think of things to talk about, because Estelle was just sitting there gulping down egg nogs and playing with the gold frog, while everyone in the place stared at her. She was wearing a Santa Claus suit which was several times her size, that Balls Off had worn the night before at a party for airline employees' families; she was wearing the white beard, and the long red and white stocking cap, and each time she would order another she'd slap the counter with her fist and shout: "Ho! Ho! Ho! Santa's ready for another load."

"A praying mantis is the same way," said Sydney. "I mean, he's just as tenacious, only the female's the voracious one. She actually eats him while he's delivering his semen."

"A cock-sucking praying mantis."

"I don't mean that kind of 'eat,' Estelle. She's a cannibal. If she gets him in a breeding cage, where he can't escape, she takes off his head."

"You go to my head," Estelle sang out.

"Some physiologists think decapitation actually increases the male's generative power."

"You're *all* a bunch of fucking masochists. Balls Off's using deodorants now," she said, "because Gracious Me won't *cohabit* with him if he hasn't used his Right Guard." She hit the bar. "Ho! Ho! —"

Sydney interrupted. "Spiders, too," he said to stop her. He signaled for another round.

"What?"

"I said spiders, female spiders go for the male's head, too."

"Bestiality," said Estelle. "Is that what you're up to at Cornell; is that why you don't have time to write?"

"I brought you some matchbooks." He fumbled in the pocket of his coat to find them.

"Are you doing sheep up in the country?"

"Here," he said, piling them in front of her. "Four different ones."

"I gave up smoking, Ranchman."

"I didn't know that."

"I was *forced* to give it up by Whale-Belly. You'd think she was giving birth to the Christ child. She says smoking pollutes the air in an apartment. You know when they did it?"

"Did what?" he said. "Who?"

"Balls Off and Gracious Me. They did it in Hawaii when I was with them. Right under my nose. I counted back. She's five months gone."

"I'm sorry, Estelle."

"I felt the thing kick in her stomach. She *made* me do it. If you ask me, she's going to give birth to a fucking ox."

"Do they want a boy or a girl?"

"What the hell do you care what they want? You didn't write once."

"I've been all wrapped up in what I'm doing. I wrote this paper," he said.

She said, "Piss off."

"It's about parthenogenesis," he said. "It's going to be published in this little quarterly."

"You know what she gave me for Christmas?"

"No."

"A makeup kit. It's so fucking fancy Emmett Kelly wouldn't be able to figure it out."

"A Gucci?"

"What?"

"I said is it something like a Gucci makeup kit? They cost a lot."

"Who said anything about a Gucci makeup kit?"

"No one did," he said. "I've just got one in the trunk of my car, that's all. I thought she might have given you one like the one I've got out in my car."

"It's a *theatrical* makeup kit," she said.

"Oh."

"I was in this play at school. *Berkeley Square*. I played

Lady Anne Pettigrew," she said, imitating an English dowager.

"You were pretty good, hmmm?"

"*She* said I was the only one with any talent, if you want to take the word of a knocked-up *Reader's Digest* subscriber. She *subscribes* to *Reader's Digest.*"

"So does my father," he said.

"So she went out and bought me this professional makeup kit for Christmas; that's the kind of an ass-licker *she* is."

"Maybe she means it, Stel."

"Oh fart. My knees knock on stage. You can hear my bones way back in the can with the toilet flushing. . . . And *she* says I ought to investigate places like Actors' Studio. She gets all that crap from watching Johnny Carson. Actors' Studio crap . . . She says maybe that'd be better for me than college."

"Maybe it would," he said.

"Anything to keep me from killing the kid after it comes down the chute," she said. "I'm going to try out for *Glass Menagerie* in February. The tryouts are being held the first week in February."

"I hope you get the part, Estelle."

"Just about the time I get the curse they're having tryouts!"

"How come you call it that?" he said.

"What am I supposed to call it?" she said.

"I just thought only older women like my mother ever

called it the curse. I thought you called it getting your period. Someone told me that once."

"Someone is full of shit, Sydney. It's the curse. That's
the only name for it," she said, "and after *Glass Menagerie*
they're doing *Summer and Smoke*."

"You're going to be busy," he said.

"I'll have to learn to pee standing up I'll be so busy."

"Right," he said. "White Christmas" was playing on
Musak, the Bing Crosby recording. Sydney looked down
and discovered that he had ripped out all the matchsticks
from the Maxwell's Plum folder and torn them in half.

Estelle said, "Did you ever read anything by Tennessee
Williams?"

"This one play: *Cat on a Hot Tin Roof.* That's all."

Estelle Kelly sighed. Then she said under her breath,
"Fuck, fuck, fuck, fuck."

"What?"

"Nada," she said.

"I wish you could come back to my mother's party with
me," he said.

"Good-bye," she said flatly.

"I didn't mean it *that* way, Estelle."

"I don't want to hang around in a screwing bar all
night, anyway," she said. "It makes me want to smoke."

"How come you don't sneak one?" he said. "If you really
wanted one, you'd sneak one."

"Please address all questions to Sarah Bernhardt, c/o
Agatha Henry, Barnard College," she said, climbing down

off the barstool. "All correspondence will be promptly answered."

It was snowing outside. East End Avenue was lighted with blue, red and green bulbs lined along terraces and up and down trees. Sydney felt a glimmering of sentimentality and was about to reach gently for her hand when Estelle Kelly said, "I hate Christmas, anyway. Everyone puts on a big act, including you and me."

"I'm not particularly acting," Sydney said.

"What do you call it then?"

"Call what?" Sydney said.

"Never mind," she said. "All the world's a stage we're going through."

Sydney tried to think of some better note to end things on. Instead he could only feel relief that they were almost to her building. As a cover-up he decided to kiss her goodnight the old meaningful way, even if she detested it.

There was a large family walking toward them, seven or eight children with a man and woman. "I can't disappoint the kiddies," Estelle said. She ran ahead of Sydney and began lurching into a litter basket, staggering into a fire hydrant, dragging through the snow in her Santa Claus suit, affecting a drunken slur as she cried out. "Yes, Virginia, there *is* a Santa Claus, but she's a souse!"

At the entrance to her apartment building she turned and looked back at Sydney, who was hurrying to catch up with her. The cold wind was whipping their faces. Her eyes were teary and her nose was red.

"Hey — if it's a boy," she shouted, "we'll name him after you!"

Then she ran inside.

Sydney drove down Lexington Avenue, mindful that he had promised M.E. he would help clean up after the party. The party would still be going. By now they would all be high and dancing, and he did not feel like forcing smiles through duty dances with Loretta Willensky, Liz, Cappy and Corita. His car wheels were spinning on the icy patches, his windshield wipers slowing up as the snow came down thicker. Christmas carols were being broadcast over WMCA along with weather bulletins and warnings to motorists that driving was unsafe.

At Twenty-second Street, Sydney saw a parking spot near the hotel and pulled into it. For a moment he sat admiring the view he faced: Gramercy Park with the giant tree in the middle, the lights blinking on it, the snow blowing drifts along the branches.

Then he locked the car and went into the hotel, headed for the bar to the right of the entrance, but turned left instead toward the phone booth.

When he heard her voice he shut the door of the phone booth.

"Is it *you?*" he said.

"Sydney?"

"Yes."

"*Sydney Skate?*"

"Is it you? I thought I'd get your mother."

"Oh wow. Sydney. I can't believe this is you."

"I've got your makeup kit in my car. I was going to tell your mother I'd drop it off."

"They're in Armonk."

"I'm right across the street."

"Do you have my makeup kit?"

"Yes. I got your card."

"I really need it because I'm going to New Orleans for intersession. God. I've never been to New Orleans. It's gross. I've never even been South."

"Are you back in Bryn Mawr?"

"Yes. I went back. I'm living in the men's dorm at Haverford. I love it there. I really freaked out, though. It was bad mesc. It was cut with meth or something. I lost my fingers in the phone kind of thing. I still get afterimages. People's faces turn into mosaics. They're afterimages. But I'm past that scene now. I'm a vegetarian."

"Are you alone, Alison?"

"I am sort of."

"Who's there? Raoul?"

"*Raoul,*" she said. "No. I'm way past that scene, too."

"I'm glad of that," Sydney said.

"People who seem super-important at a certain time make you wonder what you saw in them at all, later. You know, Sydney?"

"Yes," he said. "Then who's there?"

"No one, Sydney, but I'm sort of super-involved with someone. That's why I'm going to New Orleans for intersession. His family lives there. He's Wyatt Franklin's son."

"Whose son?"

"You don't read *Fortune* magazine. There was an article in there about him. He owns the Eastern Seaboard Signal Company. Did you ever hear of it?"

"No," Sydney said. "Who exactly owns it? Him or his father?"

"*He* doesn't own it. He rooms right above me at Haverford. Wyatt Franklin owns it. They lease burglar alarms and fire alarms. He's driving in from his uncle's right now. He's coming down from Hartford."

"Don't count on it in this storm."

"Sydney? I really need my makeup kit."

"That's why I'm calling you," he said.

She was wearing a long red velvet dress with a white lace collar, long sleeves, white lace cuffs, and nothing on underneath.

"This is really gross," she said. "I was dressed for him and now you're here enjoying it."

"Poor Wyatt Franklin's son," Sydney said, "konked out on the Merritt Parkway."

"He'll get here if he has to ski," she said. "He said he'd get here and he will. He's fantastically reliable. His father owns a seventeen-foot Boston whaler and he can run it without a crew or anything."

"Just kiss me the way you would him," said Sydney.

"I have been but God."

"What?"

"Well, I mean talking to him on the phone with you right next to me like this."

"He didn't know it."

"I don't think he did, either."

"Alison, how would he *know* it?"

"You always used to find things out, Sydney. You found out everything and it's really embarrassing when I think about it."

"Then don't think about it," he said. "I can smell Y."

"Whatever happened to Dr. Teregram?" she said.

Sydney told her. He had almost forgotten about the King, and now he remembered the day he had let the snake have her freedom. It was a short while after M.E. had stopped using code; it was when she was in St. Thomas with Liz. Had St. Thomas been the start of things with them, or had the start of things been much earlier that summer? He had always been able to chart M.E.'s affairs practically to the hour of inception, but not this new one. This new one was the first time he had been too involved with his own business to mind M.E.'s, beyond the point hers affected his. That was why he had been unable to trace the sequence of events leading up to the Thanksgiving postcard announcing: "Good news. Liz and I have decided to live together, and she'll make the move next week." It had caught him entirely by surprise.

"Do you really think it was okay to set her loose like that?" Alison said.

"She's better off than she ever was before. She's into her

own thing now," Sydney said. "She's crawled into a fissure in an expanse of rock, and slithered inward and downward a long, long distance. Her temperature is one degree lower than that of air, which makes her practically dead until next spring."

"I wish I could say that about the other Dr. Teregram," Alison said.

"Alison, I don't want to hear about the other Dr. Teregram. Please."

"She's getting forty-five an hour now out of my father. Do you know how much that is a year?"

"Alison," he said, "let's just do a lot of polymorphous-perverse things and stop sweating reality."

"Hey," she said, "I like that, Sydney."

He thought of a small angler fish called *Ceratias;* the male was just a few inches long and the female nearly three feet. When the male mated with the female, he would attach himself to a part of her forehead and bite, and the moment he bit, there was never any way to leave. Alison held on to him. He sighed and shut his eyes. His mouth was welded to her flesh; his mouth, his jaws, his teeth, his digestive canal, his fins, his gulls, and even his heart were grafted to her. Soon he would be no more than a testicle masquerading as a tiny fish, his every function dominated by the female, whose only way of communicating with him was by means of her blood vessels. Eventually, other pygmy males would attach themselves to her.

When Sydney woke it was three-thirty in the morning. Without disturbing Alison, he went into the kitchen and phoned M.E.

"Sydney!" she said. "I've been worried about you! Are you all right?"

"Sure," he said.

M.E. began to talk very fast. "I'm sorry, Sydney, that we haven't had much time together since you got home. Sydney? Liz and I've been talking and she might run down to Washington for a week or two. Then you and I can do some things together. I can pick up tickets or —"

"I'm at Alison Gray's," he interrupted. "Right over on Gramercy Park. I dropped by to return her makeup kit and I lost track of the time."

For a few seconds M.E. didn't say anything, so he said, "I'm just over here at Alison's."

M.E. said, "Estelle Kelly called to apologize for forgetting to give you your Christmas gift. When she said you'd left about eleven-thirty, we couldn't imagine what happened to you."

"I came over here."

"Why didn't you just say you had a late date with Alison?"

"I didn't know I did," he said. "I'm sorry. I was supposed to help you clean up."

"You can. Tomorrow. We haven't been doing much cleaning over here, we've been worrying instead."

"I'll clean up tomorrow," he said. Then he said, "Why should Liz go to Washington?"

"What's that?"

"I said why should Liz have to go to Washington?"

"She doesn't *have* to go to Washington."

"We could all do something together."

"All right."

"Couldn't we?"

"Yes, we could."

"Anyway, I have things I have to do. I have to write this paper on myriapods, too."

"Fine," M.E. said. "I'm just glad you're all right."

"Are *you* all right?" He could not remember ever having put that question to M.E.

"Yes," she answered. "Of course . . . Thanks . . . Why wouldn't I be?"

"I just thought I'd ask," he said. "I'm on my way home."

"Better late than never, Sydney," M.E. said.

When he hung up, Alison rushed into the kitchen. "Sydney. God. Look at the time. We fell asleep. I can't find my dress. Help me find my dress. You have to leave. You have to hurry, Sydney. He could be in the lobby right now. I'm super-scared. If I don't get to go to New Orleans for inter-session, it'll be the absolute end of me."

"Oh, I doubt that it'll be the absolute end of you, Alison," he said, following her into the living room, picking his trousers up from the floor.

"Where's my dress?"

"There." He found it beside the couch and handed it to her. "Here."

"This is freaking me out. Your socks. Put your socks on."

"Why didn't you set the alarm?" Sydney said, pushing his arms through the sleeves of his shirt, his feet into his shoes, pocketing the socks.

"*Set the alarm,*" she said flatly.

"Sometimes I think you want to be found out," he said, pulling on his boots.

"I can't put this dress back on; this dress is all wrinkles!"

"He can't get here in this snow," Sydney said. "Look out the window."

"Sydney, I don't want to hurt you, but you can see why I'd be freaked out if anything were to happen, can't you?"

"Relax," he said. "I'm dressed."

"I'm not. What am I going to do? What am I going to put on?"

"Tell him you fell asleep in your dress waiting for him."

"Yes. Good. That'll do for now." She whipped it above her shoulders and Sydney helped her pull it down over her body.

"Thank you," she said. "Oh wow. I was freaking out for a second. You don't know him. He could get here by helicopter."

Sydney buttoned his overcoat. "I wish I had something for you for Christmas," he said.

"Well, we didn't know we were going to see each other."

"Have a good time in New Orleans," he said.

She put her arms around him. She whispered "Sydney? I'm really in love."

He trudged down Irving Place through the deep snow, remembering a biology film he had seen last fall. It was a close-up, slow motion, of a male silkworm copulating with a female. The *Bombyx mori*. The female grew these minuscule yellow warts on her abdomen; the male responded to their aroma with a mad frenzy, his wings beating, whirring — his belly bending in an arc, feeling for the female opening with a wild, prancing, chaotic desire. When he found it, he held it in place with chitinous clamps, carefully, and next very gently, very softly, as the two bellies moved in together, the male became still. The beating wings fluttered down. There was no movement. Then gradually, in hard, wide beats the wings of the male flapped, for about eighty seconds, in regular cadence.

Afterward, there was almost no motion: motion barely perceptible.

Sydney turned down Nineteenth Street.

Only a slight quiver of his antennae.

The very feeblest ventral tremor.

Still attached . . . but for the time being, finished.